Stories

of Life at

Sydney Cove

'First Fleet in Sydney Cove' by marine artist, Frank Allen

Susan E Boyer

A young reader edition of 'Across Great Divides'

© Birrong Books

Published in Australia by
Birrong Books
PO Box 255, Glenbrook, NSW, 2773
www.birrongbooks.com
Email: boyer@eftel.net.au

First published by Birrong Books in 2016. Second print, March 2017.

Copyright © Susan E Boyer 2016

National Library of Australia Cataloguing-in-Publication:

Creator: Boyer, Susan E., author

Title: Stories of life at Sydney cove / Susan E Boyer

ISBN: 9781877074493 (paperback)

Readership: For ages 10 years to adult

Subjects: First Fleet, 1787-1788
           Convicts-- Australia--History--1788-1821
           Aboriginal Australians--First contact with Europeans
           Historical--Fiction.
           Sydney (N.S.W.)--History--1788-1851
           New South Wales--History--1788-1851

Dewey Number: A823.4 historical fiction

Cover design by Susan Boyer
Cover images of historical people (from left to right) are:
Sarah Leadbeater, a convict (not of the First Fleet) who married a soldier.
Lieutenant Watkin Tench who kept a journal of his adventure at Sydney & an unnamed Aboriginal man whose portrait was later found among the papers of Governor Macquarie.
These images sourced from Mitchell Library, State Library New South Wales. The harbour image is a detail from a painting, 'First Fleet in Sydney Cove' and supplied by courtesy of its creator, Frank Allen.
For illustrations throughout this book, see pages 253-254.

Teacher resources available at www.birrongbooks.com

Information for Indigenous Australian communities:

Readers, please be aware that this book contains names & images of deceased persons which in some Indigenous Australian communities may offend cultural prohibitions.

Historical background to 'Stories of Life at Sydney Cove'

Britain, by the 1780s, was a place of rapid change and upheaval. Farms and village life gave way to factories and crowded cities, and life became uncertain for many families.

People began moving from the countryside to large towns to work for low wages. It was a time when poverty led to crime, and prisons became overcrowded.

The British Government decided to send their criminals away to a distant place on the far side of the world. It seemed the perfect solution to get rid of convicts, and start a colony at the same time. Captain Phillip had the job of organising eleven ships to carry over a thousand people to a mysterious place called 'Botany Bay'. Nobody knew what to expect of the voyage or what life would be like on the edge of the known world.

'Stories of Life at Sydney Cove' is about what happened next...

All the people named in the stories really lived at Sydney Cove. You can see a list of their names on pages 250 – 251 of this book.

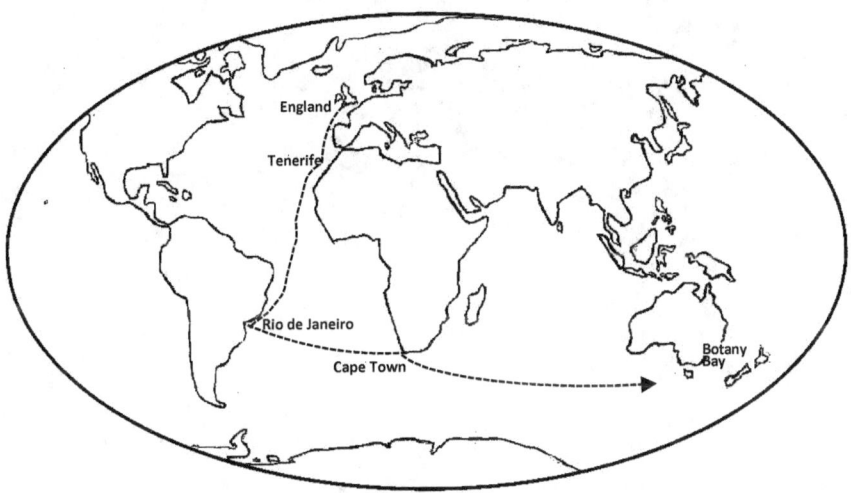

The route of the First Fleet May 1787 – January 1788

Note: The world as shown on the map above was not completely known until years after 1788.

Part 1

Voyage to the end of the world

Chapter 1

Thirteen-year-old John Hudson could not believe his luck. Life had taken a turn for the better. For several days he hadn't been woken before daylight to angry voices bellowing orders. Nor had he been rowed from the prison ship *Dunkirk* to work on the waterfront till his fingers turned blue and his lips cracked and bled from the bitter cold.

Three days ago he'd been taken by wagon to a transport ship where he learnt he was to sail to the 'ends of the earth'. Since arriving aboard *Friendship* he'd received a meal every day and he'd slept in a hammock each night. He couldn't remember a more untroubled time in his life. Sure, the convict quarters were dark and cramped, but he was used to that.

Upon transferring to the transport vessel, his filthy stinking rags had been peeled from him and replaced by government 'slops', doled out to all the male convicts. To his amazement, this included a woollen jacket, trousers, a pair of woollen stockings, a pair of shoes, two shirts, a neckerchief and hat!

If that was not enough, he realised with relief beyond words that he would never again have to re-live his worst nightmares. With the ships at sea, he would never again be forced to climb a filthy London chimneystack. He would never again be stuck inside a narrow brick flue, scraping its blackened sides of greasy muck. Transportation to the south seas did not seem such a bad thing compared to the life he had known.

****

John Hudson couldn't remember his mother or father. His earliest memories were of the poorhouse where children like him worked from morning to night in exchange for a ration of food and a place to sleep. But the wardens knew nobody checked on them and the orphans rarely knew a full belly.

Before John was eight years old and still a scrawny lad, he was sold as a 'climbing boy' to a London chimneysweep, a heartless man who drove his boys till they were exhausted. Little John hated the work but he knew it could be worse. He could be in the gutter.

During busy periods he climbed day and night up grime-encrusted chimneys barely wide enough for him. Wedged inside, with his eyes stinging and lungs wheezing, it was difficult to keep a foothold when the sides were caked with fat and soot. But it was the thought of a beating that kept his thin legs lodged in place until the sides were cleared of muck.

Clambering up into the darkness John often scraped his knees, elbows and forehead on rough, jagged brickwork. But he learnt to ignore the blood trickling down his arms or running into his eyes, just as he learnt to ignore his aching muscles and weepy sores.

He knew if he was injured, burned or blinded, he would be easily replaced. There were always younger, smaller, more nimble boys to take his job. Then he'd be back in the workhouse or out on the streets.

John learnt through necessity how to fend for himself on the streets of London. He mixed with boys in the same circumstance as himself. He learnt how to steal and resell items to stay alive. It was the only way to survive in a large city as an orphan. He knew what to say and do to avoid trouble...that is until the day, at the age of nine years old, he was caught.

****

John Hudson was arrested for burglary and sent to Newgate Prison. He was accused of stealing a linen shirt, silk stockings and two aprons from a house in the middle of the night. A maid discovered the items were missing the following morning, and sooty little footprints were noticed by a window.

During the court case, a witness reported that John Hudson had brought clothes to his pawnshop to sell them. The boy said his mother had sent him and the clothes belonged to his father. But his grubby appearance raised suspicion.

Another witness said that later on the day of the robbery, a pistol was found inside a stocking with other clothes and John was seen near the stash. He was held till a policeman arrived but questioned in the meantime.

'Do you know anything about this?'

'I dunno nuthin',' John mumbled. Rough hands shook him.

'Then we'll fetch somebody that will make you know!' John tried to stay unmoved by the threat, but his nerves gave way.

'There was another boy,' he blurted. He said the other boy broke the window and got into the house.

'I 'ad nuthin to do with it.'

But during the court case, when his bare little foot was compared with the imprint taken at the crime scene, he admitted he'd been in the house too. The judge peered down at him.

'How old are you?'

'Goin' on nine.' John kept his head down and his answers short.

'What business were you bred up in?'

'None, sometimes a chimney sweeper.'

'Have you any father or mother?'

'Dead,' John replied simply.

'How long ago?'

'I dunno.'

The judge was clearly moved by the sad little boy hunched before him. He addressed the court.

'The boy's confession was made under fear, so I do not think it should be allowed as evidence. At the most, it only proves he was in the house and he might have got in after daybreak...'

He sighed heavily. 'I think it would be too hard to find a boy of his tender age guilty of the burglary.'

Then speaking to everyone in the courtroom, the judge continued.

'One would wish to snatch such a boy, if possibly, from destruction for he will only return to the same kind of life and continue to be an instrument in the hands of very bad people, who make use of boys of this sort to rob houses.'

After a pause, the judge gave his verdict[1].

'John Hudson is found guilty of a felony[2], but not of the burglary. He is sentenced to transportation for seven years.'

Since his conviction at the age of nine, John had endured years of misery in prison and aboard the hulk, *Dunkirk.* His experience of life on the streets of London had helped him survive that awful period...until he arrived aboard the transport vessel, *Friendship*, at the age of thirteen.

****

That life, John's 'old' life, was behind him now. As the ships prepared to sail into the vast oceans of the world, he really had no idea where he was heading. A faraway land, somewhere, was all he knew. They were going to start a colony, whatever that meant. It didn't really matter to young John Hudson. He'd heard that at the place called 'Botany Bay' there were no towns, no streets, no buildings...or rooftops with chimneystacks.

---

[1] decision of a court
[2] breaking the law, a crime

Chapter 2

1787, Aboard *Friendship* before sailing

Lieutenant Ralph Clark was a young married marine. Eager to advance his career, he had volunteered for duty at Botany Bay. He watched the female convicts clamber one by one up the damp rope ladder and onto the deck of *Friendship*. Several had little ones with them and he felt a flicker of resentment. It didn't seem fair that these shameful women were allowed to bring infants, when he so desperately wished his wife and little Ralphie, were sailing with him. But his request had been refused on the grounds that family life would interfere with his military duties.

If only he could see them before sailing, but even that was denied him!

He expressed his bitterness in his diary:

> *I can never forgive the unkindness of the captain in refusing me leave to sleep out of the ship last night. Oh did he love as I do, he would never have refused me.*

The following weeks were too hectic with preparation for sailing to write in his journal, but as the time approached, he wrote again:

> *Oh my God – all my hopes are over of seeing my beloved wife and son…I never should have thought of leaving the best of women and the most sweetest of boys but to Botany Bay I must go.*

Not many of the convicts aboard the departing ships could express their feelings in writing like Ralph Clark. However, their hearts still ached for the loved ones they would never see or hold again.

Aboard *Friendship* Henry Kable, a strongly built, red-haired youth knew his situation was exceptional. He had escaped death by hanging, unlike the other men caught robbing a house with him. He was the only male convict from Norwich Prison and he was the only one who had actually begged to go to Botany Bay. Amazingly, details of what happened to him had appeared in several British newspapers.

****

Some years earlier...

The story of Henry's journey to Botany Bay began with Susannah, a young woman also sentenced to hang for burglary. Like Henry, her penalty was changed to 'transportation across the seas' instead. While confined in Norwich Castle prison they fell in love and desperately wanted to get married, but the prison authorities said no. Prisoners had no such rights under British law. The following year, after baby Henry junior was born, they begged once more to become husband and wife. But the authorities again denied their request. Their future did not look promising.

Norwich Castle Prison

Then, when baby Henry was five months old, something happened to change the course of their lives.

****

The time had come for the British Government to assemble convicts for the planned penal settlement on the far side of the world. And when a letter arrived at Norwich Prison ordering the removal of female prisoners to Plymouth Harbour to await transportation, Susannah's name was on the list.

At first, the announcement stunned the young parents to their core. They'd known the time would come for their transfer to a place of exile, but they always imagined they would stay together. When the shock of Susannah's approaching removal finally sank in, the pair went into a frantic state. Henry knew he couldn't bear separation from Susannah and his baby. He must do something.

'How will I manage without you,' Susannah sobbed, terrified at the thought of sailing alone to a distant and unknown land.

'Don't fret,' Henry whispered. 'I will do everything in my power to be with you and our dear boy.'

Henry knew he needed the support of someone with influence so he sought the aid of a local squire[3]. He begged the gentleman to contact and explain his situation to Lord Sydney, the man in charge of convict administration. He asked for permission to go to the place of banishment 'Botany Bay' with the mother of his child.

His appeal was so heart wrenching that the squire agreed to write a letter on Henry's behalf.

---

[3] landowner

Within days a reply came stating the request could not be granted. Henry and Susannah felt empty and hopeless.

****

The time arrived when the female prisoners, including Susannah, gathered their few belongings and reluctantly climbed onto an open wagon, under the guard of a prison warden named John Simpson.

'Best brace yerselves – t'will be a long passage,' the guard warned.

The journey to Plymouth Harbour they learnt would take more than three days. Susannah hugged her baby close to protect him from the biting wind and cushion his little body against the rough ride.

The cart rumbled through the cold and rain, stopping only for a change of horses. The prisoners were then given a piece of bread, a cup of water and a chance to visit the outhouse.

Even when the cart paused, the icy air whirled around the hunched bodies, but Susannah hardly felt it. She was numb with despair. The vision of Henry's face in their last moment together cut her like a knife. 'If it wasn't for my little Henry,' she thought, 'there'd be no reason to go on now.'

As the group sped southward, little did Susannah realise there was so much worse to come.

****

The wagon wheels finally ground to a halt near the waterfront and the women were ordered out of the cart and toward a timber wharf. Susannah's legs felt painfully cramped from the long journey but she picked her way cautiously along the slippery jetty, holding baby Henry close. The women were directed into a rowboat and taken alongside a rundown old ship where they would be kept until the transport ships were ready to take them.

After waiting in the open boat for hours in the freezing November air, Susannah and the other women were ordered aboard the prison hulk *Dunkirk*, escorted by the gaoler, John Simpson. As soon as the captain saw the babe in Susannah's arms, he checked his list.

'I've no order to take a child,' he growled. 'Where's the proper form?'

'I have no such form,' John Simpson quickly cut in. 'But be assured, I had instructions to deliver both mother and babe.'

'Without the proper form, you can take the child away,' the captain snarled, turning his back.

'Please, no!' begged Susannah. 'Don't take my baby from me!'

'Take the wretch below,' he called over his shoulder.

As John Simpson followed the captain and tried to reason with him, Susannah became hysterical. She could see the man was not going to change his mind.

Finally, little Henry was pulled from his mother's arms as she was dragged away sobbing uncontrollably.

'I can't live without my baby!' she cried as she was led to the convict quarters. 'Please!' she called to Simpson.

Shaken by the cold-heartedness of the captain, John Simpson had no choice but to return to shore with the baby.

By the time he reached the wharf, he knew what he had to do. The scene of the mother's agony had affected him so intensely he felt he must make an urgent application to Lord Sydney, in person.

Simpson set off in the first coach for London, carrying little Henry all the way on his knee, stopping at inns to feed him along the journey.

When he arrived in London, he placed the baby in the care of a trusted friend and continued to the offices of Lord Sydney. There was no time to waste.

'I'm afraid, sir, you do not have an appointment,' the clerk frowned. 'His Lordship is not available.'

But John Simpson was a man on a mission and would not be stopped. He pushed past the clerk into one of the offices where he found one of Lord Sydney's personal secretaries. He quickly told the whole story of Henry and Susannah's sad tale with such feeling that the man promised to do all in his power to help their cause.

'But I fear it will be impossible to see Lord Sydney for several days,' the assistant added.

'Then I'm willing to wait in the hall for a chance to see him. In the meantime, I beg you to prepare an order for the return of the child to its mother so I can bid His Lordship to sign it.'

John Simpson hadn't waited long when he saw Lord Sydney descend a staircase and he immediately approached him with his request. At first the government minister was outraged that anyone should address him in such an uninvited manner and refused to listen. But Simpson hurriedly related the reason for his call, describing the scene of misery he had recently witnessed.

'Your Lordship, I fear that in this very instant, the unhappy woman in the wildness of her despair, may end her life.'

Lord Sydney was greatly affected by Simpson's story and impressed by his kindness on behalf of helpless prisoners.

'I must commend your humanity Mr Simpson. I will ensure the child is restored to its mother at once.'

Encouraged by this, Simpson made a further appeal that the father of the child also be allowed to join Susannah. To his delight, Lord Sydney gave his approval.

'I will instruct my secretary straightaway to inform the woman of the success of your application. And you must return to Norwich to communicate my consent to the father of the child.'

When Simpson told Henry Kable everything that had happened over the past days, he beamed with gratitude.

'Lord Sydney will not regret his charity. I will do all I can to be useful in the new colony,' Henry promised.

By the time Simpson delivered Henry Kable to Plymouth Dock, he had been on the road a further three days and nights with little sleep. But the delight of witnessing the family reunion outweighed any difficulty he'd endured. He described his emotion in a letter to his friend.

November 16, 1786

Dear Sir,

It is with great pleasure that I inform you of the safe arrival of my charges to Plymouth. I cannot describe the joy of the mother receiving her infant and her intended husband. The tears that flowed from their eyes with the innocent smile of the babe and the sight of the mother who had saved her milk for it, drew tears from my eyes.

It was with great regret that I parted with the child after travelling with it on my lap upwards of 700 miles backwards and forwards. But the blessing I received at the different inns on the road have rewarded me well.

Your humble servant,
John Simpson

700 miles = 1,100 kilometres

After almost two weeks of painful separation, Henry and Susannah were together with their baby boy. But their story did not end there.

Simpson's actions on behalf of the convict couple bound for 'the ends of the earth' attracted British media attention. Readers were amazed by the tale. The story came to the attention of a wealthy lady who was so affected by the story that she organised public donations for the couple. The contributions amounted to the sum of twenty pounds - about four times the value of the goods Susannah had stolen to land her in prison. A crate of donated items was loaded onto one of the transport ships for the benefit of the couple once they arrived in Botany Bay. That crate would become an important part of the Kable's ongoing story.

It had been an unbelievable turn-around for Henry and Susannah. After spending six months aboard the prison hulk *Dunkirk* in Plymouth Harbour, they were sent aboard *Friendship*, one of the eleven ships departing for Botany Bay. The transports had separate quarters for male and female convicts but Henry hoped he could keep a look out for his family.

****

Finally, before daylight on May 13th 1787, Henry felt a shudder go through the ship as wind filled its sails and the anchor was raised. The transport ships were beginning the long voyage with the convicts chained securely below deck to prevent an uprising or escape.

Over seven hundred convicts and their marine guards were beginning a journey to a strange land on the edge of the known world. It would be the largest expedition in European history.

None of the convicts knew what to expect of the voyage. They had no knowledge of the world. They had no idea of the distance they would travel, or of their destination. They'd heard that dark skinned native people lived at Botany Bay, and that a strange leaping animal called 'kangaroo' carried its baby in a pocket at the front of its body. Besides that, they had no idea what wild creatures lived there, but rumours abounded.

Reports spread that enormous snakes and spiders the size of dinner plates existed in the regions to the south and that flesh-eating animals and vicious, deadly reptiles prowled the landscape.

In addition to those awful rumours, a report printed in a London newspaper, with the heading 'The Botany Bay scheme', called their destination a 'place of cannibals':

GENERAL EVENING POST

November 9, 1786
The Botany Bay Scheme
The proposed settlement in those regions of the South is thought to be the habitation of cannibals.

Could such a report possibly be true?
How would they survive such a place?

Like all the convicts, Henry and Susannah knew nothing about their place of banishment. But they did know they would be together, and that was all that mattered to them.

Chapter 3

May 1787 - Aboard *Lady Penrhyn,* at sea

As the ship rolled and pitched thirteen-year-old Elizabeth Hayward felt another wave of nausea wash over her. She squeezed her eyelids tight but the blackness brought the reality of her situation even more intensely to her ears and nostrils. The groans were constant, the smell overpowering.

She thought again of her stupidity in stealing from her factory employer.

How did she think she would possibly get away with it?

It had been a foolish attempt to better her circumstances but instead she had ended up on a convict ship with a hundred other female prisoners. Last night she hadn't slept a wink. Despite being crammed shoulder to shoulder, the icy air had seeped through the boards freezing her bones till they felt they would snap. At least they were no longer in chains.

The ship lurched again causing a chorus of shrieks and curses. Elizabeth wanted to leap up the ladder, bang on the hatch and yell,

'Let me out of here!'

But she sat silently, hugging her small thin body, peering through the gloom at her travel companions.

Elizabeth already knew a number of the women well. She'd watched some of them work their charms on the guards at Newgate Prison to get extra food and blankets. She'd seen them steal from old and weak prisoners and then overheard them brag about it.

However, she'd also heard women declaring their innocence and mothers whose sad eyes told their distress at leaving their children. She'd seen them sobbing about the sorry state they'd made for themselves. Yet all the women aboard *Lady Penrhyn* knew it was too late for regret.

She tried to push images of her weeks in Newgate Prison from her mind but such memories were not easy to erase. Drunken men and women chained to the walls to suppress their violent outbursts, while others slumped on the damp stone floor, too weak to offer any threat.

****

Two months earlier...

Elizabeth was taken from the prison to the Old Bailey Courthouse for trial. When she was led into the courtroom with its stately columns and rows of glaring men in grey wigs and black gowns, Elizabeth felt her legs give way. In all her thirteen years, she had never been in a place so grand, yet so daunting.

As witnesses were questioned and evidence produced, all she could do was keep her head down and hope to high heaven, those stern men would show her mercy.

But it had all come out - how she'd stolen a gown, a bonnet and a cloak, taken them to a pawnshop and sold them to a woman named Constant, who was also standing trial for receiving the stolen goods.

When the court declared there was no evidence against Constant and pronounced her 'Not Guilty', Elizabeth felt the tiniest flicker of hope. But her own verdict had boomed loud and clear across the courtroom.

'Elizabeth Hayward - Guilty!'

Her punishment was 'transportation', which she understood meant she was banished to a faraway place for an unimaginably long time.

****

As the *Lady Penrhyn* began her epic voyage, arguing erupted over trivial things in the crowded convict quarters. The tough, hard-edged women brought their vicious habits from Newgate prison and were punished for stealing, fighting and abusive language.

Others amongst the prisoners were quiet and docile and kept their past to themselves, while some loved to talk. Dorothy Handland won hands down as the ultimate story-teller. She also had the distinction of being the oldest convict.

Unlike most of the women, sentenced for stealing of some kind, Dorothy proudly announced that her sentence was for something completely out of the ordinary.

'Perjury! I was put away for perjury!' she declared triumphantly.

'What's perjury?' Young Elizabeth Hayward was intrigued.

'Purposely telling lies to a magistrate in court,' someone piped up.

'It was just tellin' a few stories, that's all. Tryin' te better me lot.'

****

Dorothy Handland was listed in the ship's records as eighty-two years old, and described as a 'dealer in old clothes'. Her wrinkly face, stringy hair and missing teeth reflected her tough life. She was in fact younger than her listed age but, she was happy to use her tired old appearance to her advantage.

Old Dot was the greatest storyteller Elizabeth Hayward had ever heard. She had the knack of getting her audience hooked on a tale because they were so wild and detailed. She told stories of the characters she'd encountered in her long life and the antics they got up to. Her listeners suspected all the stories were about her. She swore every word was true but when questioned she often got her facts confused. However it helped pass the time listening to old Dot.

Nobody aboard *Lady Penrhyn* was surprised that her 'tall tales' had landed old Dorothy in Newgate Prison. Nor did they think they had heard the true version of events.

****

One year earlier...

Dorothy Handland had gone to a magistrate's office clutching a dirty cloth to dab her streaming tears to add drama to her invented story.

'I've been robbed! I've been robbed of everything I 'ave in the world. I 'ave nothin' but what I stand up in. I know the man that robbed me and I want a warrant.'

But her scheme had backfired. Later in court the true story came out as witnesses were questioned.

In the courtroom, the man from the magistrate's office said her original story had been such a blundering tale, he'd told her she would need more proof. Then, he told the court, she'd said she would pay him well, if he helped her. He said he had refused her offer.

Another witness was called and questioned. She described herself as an old clothes seller who had known Dorothy for sixteen years.

'Did she talk to you about the man she says robbed her?'

'She said she'd give me money if I'd say I saw a man come out of 'er place with a great bundle wrapped in a sheet.'

'Did you see this man carry a bundle, as she asked you to swear?'

'I did not. I told her it was false, and I'd be hanged if I swore so.'

'No more questions.'

The result of Dorothy Handland's court hearing was not surprising.

'Guilty of willful perjury at the Old Bailey - sentenced to transportation for seven years.'

****

In the gloom of Lady Penrhyn's hold, with her audience gathered, Dorothy re-told her story, each time adding extra details.

'I was crying, and breaking my heart in the courtroom, I was.
I said I'd be obliged to take charity after being robbed, I did.'

Her performances broke the boredom for some. Others rolled their eyes. Some of the female convicts didn't join in the chitchat at all.

Isabella Rawson, a convict twice Elizabeth Hayward's age, sat helpless and alone, staring into space much of the time. Her baby was almost due. Elizabeth knew Isabella from Newgate Prison and their court appearances had been on the same day at the Old Bailey.

****

Months earlier…

At her trial, Isabella's swollen belly was already noticeable. During questioning, it came out that Isabella Rawson had been a servant in the home of a wealthy barrister. In evidence, her master said she had always behaved exceedingly well, and was trusted with keys to the cellar where surplus household items were stored in chests.

But temptation got in the way and she had helped herself to the contents of the trunks. In court, her employer gave his account coldly.

'She begged I would forgive her. She fell down on her knees, and pleaded for mercy. She said she was in distress.'

'What was your response?'

'I told her she had no reason to beg for mercy because she had behaved ungrateful.'

The next witness was the barrister's wife. She retold the incident in detail and with clear resentment.

'In the morning I went down to the cellar and the prisoner, seeing me go toward the trunks to open them, immediately fell on her knees, and cried out, "Madam, I have robbed you. You need not open the trunks for I've taken out all the bed curtains. Madam, do what you please with me, kill me, I deserve it," she said to me.'

'You deserve no mercy from me, I told her.'

Turning attention to the stolen goods, the cross-examiner asked,

'And the curtains? Did she say what she had done with them?'

'She said she had pawned them herself, telling the pawnbroker they were her own,' said the barrister's wife.

'And what have you to say for yourself?' the judge asked, looking toward the prisoner.

Isabella's shame-filled eyes glistened as she tried to steady her voice.
'I leave myself to the mercy of the Court.'

The verdict was given. 'Guilty - to be transported for seven years.'

Tears had streamed down Isabella's cheeks as she bent forward, her small hands stroking her belly.

What had she done? How would she care for her baby now?

May 1787 - Aboard *Lady Penrhyn,* at sea

Isabella's tiny daughter came into the world on a thin straw mattress in the dingy surrounds of the ship's hold, two weeks after the fleet sailed. Her birth caused joy and sadness in the convict quarters where the baby brought tender smiles, and at the same time, tears of sorrow from the mothers of children lost, or left behind.

Thirteen-year-old Elizabeth Hayward had watched Isabella's face twisting with pain and decided she would never have a baby if it hurt that much. But when she saw the baby's little rosebud lips and tiny fingers and toes, she decided that maybe one day she *would* have her own.

Isabella struggled to keep her baby alive, but her little girl died a week after her birth. The women were permitted on deck for the funeral service where they stood with bowed heads as the baby's tiny body, wrapped in a small canvas cover, was dropped into the vast ocean.

Two days later, the unhappy event was overshadowed by the fleet's arrival at the island of Tenerife, their first port since leaving England.

The convicts were then locked below deck, but received a welcome treat of fresh beef and vegetables. Isabella however was not interested in food.

Nothing mattered any more. What was there to live for now?

The other women saw Isabella's bent body alone in the corner, and they whispered their concern for her.

'What can we do to ease the poor lass's heartache?' they said.

They knew that Isabella was one of the few among them who could read and write. Most of them could only mark their name with an X.

Maybe there was a way to rekindle her interest in living.

Young Elizabeth Hayward approached her gently, not sure if she wanted the help she was about to ask of Isabella.

'Bella, when we gets to where we goin', will ye show me how to do me letters?' Isabella looked up blankly and nodded.

A seed of hope had been sown. Little by little, as weeks went by, Isabella gradually regained strength and began to see a reason to live. There were at least eight children of convict women aboard *Lady Penrhyn,* ranging from a few months old to eight years. She could improve their lives. The new colony would need teachers.

****

By mid-June the fleet left Tenerife and headed into the tropical zone. The air became hot and humid above deck but it was stifling in the airless confines of the ship's hold. The women could hardly breathe. Some of them fainted and had fits. Old Dorothy Handland thought she was going to die.

But there were moments of wonder too. One morning the convicts were allowed on deck for air, and as young Elizabeth climbed the ladder and went through the hatch, she was stunned by the blueness of the sky. Squinting against its brightness, she headed for the rail of the ship where she witnessed an amazing sight.

At first she thought she was seeing birds diving and soaring near the surface of the water. But as she stared, she realised they were fish. Fish with wings!

'Flying fish!' she pointed and called to anyone who would listen.

'Aye, lass. That's exactly what they are, flying fish,' a sailor nodded as if it were a common sight. Other convicts hurried to the rail, gaping at the fish flapping above the water parallel to the ship.

'Well I'll be…! Well I never…! Wonders will never cease,' came the responses from the women.

As if the ocean had decided to put on a marine show especially for them, a much larger creature appeared, jumping out of the water to a great height.

'They'd be dolphins.' The same seaman told them. 'It's a sign of good luck it is, when dolphins swim with the ship.'

Then in mid-July they were told they were about to cross a line.

'The Equator, it's called. It's a line that divides the world ye see. There's the top 'alf where England is, and when we cross the Equator, we be on t'other side.'

Elizabeth thought they must be close to the end of their journey if they were already on the other side of the world. Like all the convicts, she had no idea how far they had to travel. In reality, they still had half a year to endure at sea.

Chapter 4

July - August 1787 - Aboard *Charlotte*, at sea

Lieutenant Watkin Tench considered the convicts in his charge. Other officers had complained about the 'rascals and wretches' on the other transports, but he disagreed with their opinion. The convicts aboard *Charlotte* had so far not given any trouble. He was relieved when early in the voyage Captain Phillip, the fleet's leader, directed that the convicts could be released from their chains, if it was safe to do so. Tench had been pleased to allow the prisoners some freedom below deck and supervised periods on the open decks.

Little did he suspect that as the ship made its way across the Atlantic Ocean, a daring scheme was underway in the convict quarters.

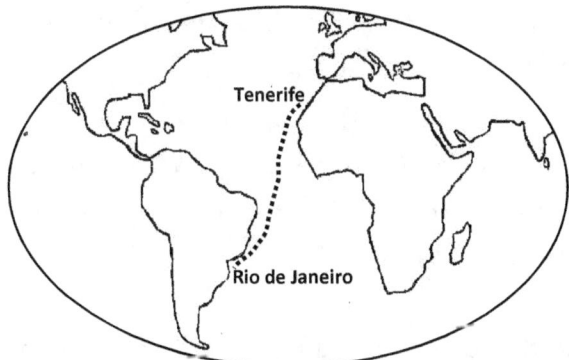

The mastermind and talent behind the plan was a convict working quietly below deck between Tenerife and the port of Rio de Janeiro. When the ships anchored in Rio's scenic harbour in early August, the plot was discovered when a Portuguese trading boat came alongside *Charlotte* to sell fruit.

Stories of Life at Sydney Cove

As the English officers paid for the produce, it came to light that some of the coins were fake. John White, the doctor aboard *Charlotte*, was embarrassed by the incident and staggered by the production.

How had the coins been made without discovery?
How was such a complex process possible?

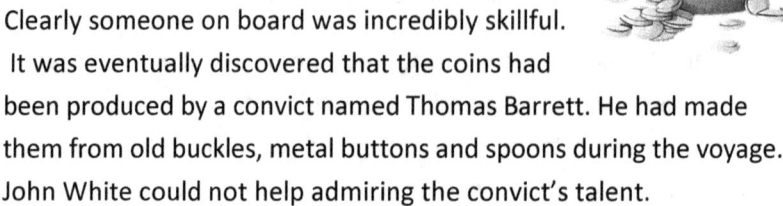

Clearly someone on board was incredibly skillful. It was eventually discovered that the coins had been produced by a convict named Thomas Barrett. He had made them from old buckles, metal buttons and spoons during the voyage. John White could not help admiring the convict's talent.

Barrett had been sentenced for stealing, but it was never discovered how or where he learnt his coin-making skills. It was clear the fake coins couldn't have been produced without the aid of at least one guard who saw the profit in such a scheme. John White, quite stunned by the affair, wrote in his journal:

> *How he managed this business without discovery is a matter of inexpressible surprise to me.*
>
> *A guard was constantly guarding the hatchway, making it impossible for either fire or metal to be taken into their quarters. The cleverness that Barrett used to complete such a complicated process, gave me a high opinion of his skill.*

Further investigation uncovered the guard involved in the scheme, and he was punished with a flogging. But it was Thomas Barret who intrigued Doctor John White. He could see how Barrett's skill could be used once they arrived in Botany Bay.

The fleet stayed at Rio for a month, then headed across the Atlantic Ocean, and arrived in Cape Town, South Africa in mid-October.

Chapter 5

November 1787 - The ships sail into unchartered ocean

At Cape Town some convicts were moved to other ships to make way for the hundreds of animals taken on board for the new colony. When Susannah and her baby transferred to *Charlotte*, Henry Kable was uneasy about the separation, and worried about their safety.

As the ships headed into the Indian Ocean, they were leaving civilisation behind to cross the longest stretch of ocean so far. They were heading into a vast unknown. Cape Town had been the final place to buy food, and their last chance to send letters home. Anxious about what lay ahead, Lieutenant Collins wrote in his journal:

November 1787

All communication with families and friends now cut off, we are leaving the world behind us, to enter a state unknown.

Sailing from Cape Town, Captain Phillip had no idea what dangers awaited his fleet of eleven ships. There was no map for their route.

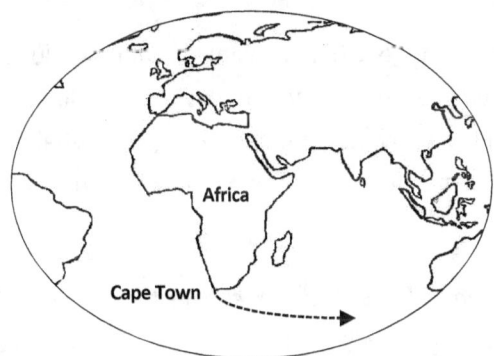

Soon after leaving Africa, a strong headwind slowed the ships' progress. Captain Phillip reduced everyone's daily water ration in case they ran out before reaching Botany Bay.

The temperature started to drop and sheep taken on board at Cape Town began to die of cold and disease. At the end of November, they were hit by gale-force winds that rocked the ships violently. When some convicts suffered an attack of dysentery, the stink of vomit and overturned toilet buckets was unbearable below deck.

Then without warning, the wind stopped and a thick fog surrounded the ships. There was no wind power to drive them forward. For the convicts locked below, the stillness was more nerve-racking than the violent pitching of the ship they had experienced days before. It felt like they were trapped in a floating coffin.

At one point, crew aboard *Lady Penrhyn* yelled urgently that they could see the outline of an enormous rock directly ahead of the ship's course. Fortunately, it was a false alarm. An officer wrote:

> *But on a second view, it proved to be a dead whale of an enormous size. Its back was a great height out of the water and at first had the appearance of a rock, as it was covered over with sea birds.*

At other times, huge whales swam alarmingly close to the ships. One night two enormous creatures swam directly under *Lady Penrhyn* and the convicts reported feeling the whales pass beneath. They feared and imagined being swallowed alive by the sea monsters.

After everything so far, would they survive the last part of the journey?

Midway across the southern Indian Ocean, the air turned icy. Storms and rough seas again tossed the convicts about below deck. The hatches had to be kept closed, and with no fresh air circulating, the smell of seasickness worsened and their misery increased. They were still over a thousand miles from Botany Bay. But by the first week of January 1788 they had reached the south-east cape of 'Terra-Australis' and began heading north along the coast.

Then, just as they thought they had endured the worst conditions possible, they were hit again by horrific storms. Only weeks before arriving in Botany Bay they suffered a terrifying night as torrential rain and hail lashed the ships so violently that the women's quarters of *Lady Penrhyn* began filling with water.

Expecting to drown as swirling water swept them off their feet, convicts prayed for their lives as forked lightning and booming thunder surrounded the ships. Gale-force winds ripped some of the ships' sails to pieces.

But against the odds they survived. At last, after eight months at sea, they were nearing the end of their long, harsh journey.

Botany Bay was only days away.

****

The convicts knew that once the ships anchored, they would be under guard below deck to prevent an uprising or escape. But that did not stop some of them making daring plans.

Aboard *Lady Penryn*, thirty-year-old convict Ann Smith had boasted to her companions during the voyage that she would escape as soon as they landed. The other women wondered if she would actually follow through with her crazy plan when the time came. They had glimpsed the coastline of this alien land during periods on deck. All that was there, as far as the eye could see, was wilderness...and threads of smoke rising in the distance.

Were they the fires of the cannibals they had heard about?

****

As the ships approached their destination, the convicts, marines and officers aboard the ships were not the only ones about to witness strange new sights. Other people – the people already living on the coast – were about to be drawn into the drama of the First Fleet.

The people living on the shores of Botany Bay were completely unaware that eleven ships were heading their way. They had no idea that over a thousand people were about to sail into their lives. They, and their families before them, had lived in their secluded homeland isolated from rest of the world for thousands of years.

They had no idea that their ancient existence was about to be shattered.

Chapter 6

January 1788, 'Kamay' (Botany Bay)

On the shoreline of Kamay, a gathering of friends and family enjoys the still summer heat. Some are diving for crayfish while others fish with spears. Another group prepares the fire for their seafood meal as children play nearby. It is an ordinary day.

The peace is suddenly broken by a sharp call from the ridge above.

'Warra, warra!' (Go away!)

Heads turn. There is a buzz of activity as someone points out to sea. Others run to see what the fuss is about. Curiosity turns to uncertainty as the group reaches the headland.

Peering across the distant waves, they see something strange approaching; something they have never seen before.

Some of the older ones become agitated. They *have* seen this sight before. In their customary way they begin recounting the arrival of strangers long ago in their *murry nowee (very big canoe)*.

****

The story, though spoken with different words, told how something similar arrived from the sea, like a floating island with great white wings. When it reached their bay, strange people put smaller boats on the water and came ashore. The visitors were odd creatures; their bodies hidden, their faces were as pale as sand. They offered useless gifts and took fishing spears in return.

They tried to communicate with strange words and sounds but they couldn't speak properly. Soon the visitors returned to their boat and left the way they came. It was a great relief to see them go.

****

That was many seasons ago, but it seems it is happening again. The group watches, as the largest *nowee* ever seen, approaches from the sea. As it gets closer, the natives try to make out the creatures peering back at them across the water. One of the older men tells the group to be wary of the visitors. Others are following his lead, brandishing their spears and shouting.

'Warra, warra!' (Go away!)

But the shouting and gestures make no difference. The object is getting closer.

There is discussion about how to deal with the visitors and different ideas and opinions are exchanged.

Everyone knows something very significant is about to happen. This day will be remembered. This story will be related to children and grandchildren for generations to come.

This day would be the end...and the beginning.

Chapter 7

18th January 1788, Botany Bay

Captain Phillip arrived in Botany Bay aboard the fastest ship of the fleet, *HMS Supply*. He was a day or so ahead of the other vessels. As Governor of the planned colony, he wanted to prepare for any unexpected challenges.

As he sailed into the bay, a group of natives appeared on the south shore, shouting and making gestures that did not look welcoming. Observing this, he directed his crew towards the northern side.

Seeing some natives watching them with interest, the Governor decided to launch a rowboat and go to meet them. As the British men neared the beach, two of the natives came close to the water's edge talking loudly and pointing to another part of the shore to indicate that another place was better for landing their boat. As the Governor didn't sense anything threatening in their voices or gestures, they rowed closer.

In the meantime one of the officers made signs that they needed water by putting his hat over the side of the boat and pretending to scoop water to his mouth. The natives, immediately understanding his meaning, pointed and walked to the westward.

'Diee warra.'(That way.) A man shouted, showing the direction.

'Budyeree bado!' (Good water.) Another man called, pointing to a particular place.

Upon landing and finding drinking water, the Governor made signs to thank the natives and offered presents but they were clearly hesitant about coming nearer. When they finally did come close enough to accept gifts, it was with signs of fear and uncertainty. They were unsure who, or what, they were dealing with. It was clear they'd never seen such a strange creature before.

Captain Arthur Phillip

The following morning the same group of natives appeared on the shore with additional friends, and when Arthur Phillip went to meet them, they approached without hesitation and without their weapons.

So, by the time the whole fleet anchored in Botany Bay, Governor Phillip had already met with one group of native people. So far though, he had only met men. The women and children were kept at a safe distance, protected from danger by their warriors.

Chapter 8

20th January 1788, Botany Bay

As the other ships reached Botany Bay one after another, more first-time face-to-face meetings took place between nervous groups of white and black men.

****

George Worgan was a young doctor aboard *HMS Sirius*. As they sailed into Botany Bay, he was feeling excited and a little scared. He was eager to explore the new surroundings, and curious about the native people he had heard about. He could just make out some figures on the distant shoreline.

As the white men leaned over the ship's rail searching the shore for a suitable landing place, the black men in like manner, studied the huge approaching object. Both groups were equally inquisitive about the scene before them.

George wanted to remember everything he saw to share with his family later and wrote about his first experiences of the new land in a letter to his brother Richard in England.

As we were sailing in, we saw 8 or 10 natives sitting on rocks and talking very intently to each other and at the same time pointing towards the ships.

They were entirely naked, and each of them had long spears and a short stick in their hands.

He wondered what would happen when his party landed.

****

As the ships drew closer, a group of natives seeing the sight for the first time tried to make out the strange creatures moving around on them. They appeared to be men but maybe they were something else. Maybe they were animals of some kind.

'Mee diee?' (What are they?) They looked to each other for ideas.

'Boo-roo-min?' (Possums?) A native man asked and shrugged.

Faced with such a dilemma, they went into the forest and lit a fire to discuss the baffling scene they had just witnessed.

If we ignore the strange beings, maybe they will go away.

But on seeing a small boat lowered over the side of the ship and coming towards the beach, the people on the shore knew they must decide on their next move.

'Nal-lar, barua,' (Look, they're coming near) a native man called.

We must find out their intention...then we can decide what to do. We must go and meet them. We must show no fear.

The natives came out of the forest and walked along the beach at a short distance from the water's edge.

****

George Worgan described what happened when the party, including the Governor, landed on the beach and met this group of native men for the first time:

> *The Governor held up some beads, red cloth and other baubles and made signs for them to advance. But they were very shy and timid and would not come closer.*
>
> *The Governor showed them his musket and then laid it on the ground, advancing alone towards them.*
>
> *Now seeing that he had nothing in his hands like a weapon, one of the oldest of the natives gave his spears to a younger and approached to meet the Governor making signs for the things to be laid on the ground.*
>
> *After various methods to impress them that we meant no harm, they began to show a confidence and became very familiar and curious about our clothes, feeling the coat, waistcoat, and even the shirt and on seeing one of the gentlemen pull off his hat, they all gave a loud whoop.*

But the native men weren't the only ones who were curious.

The British men were amazed by the black men's body decorations. George described the painted designs on their bodies made with red and white clay, and raised scars across their chests and upper arms, cut in particular lines and patterns.

Eventually one of the native men was curious and confident enough to approach one of the officers and grab hold of his hair-braid, plaited at the back of his neck.

The daring young fellow then called to his friends to come and look at it and feel it. George told his brother this caused another loud whoop, and other displays of astonishment.

For the white men, another decoration that caught their attention, was the bone that some of the natives wore through a hole in their nose.

By this stage the two groups of men were feeling more comfortable with each other. So the native men, wanting to know if the white men had similar holes for decoration, began trying to push twigs and small bones through the visitors' noses.

George told his brother, the natives laughed heartily as they allowed the white men to put caps on their heads and drape coloured cloth over their shoulders. He also wrote in his letter:

Animal's bones, stuck in their hair with gum, is another of their elegant ornaments. When we looked at these decorations to admire them, some good-natured fellows immediately pulled them off and presented them to us.

Stories of Life at Sydney Cove

At this early meeting everyone seemed to be having a good time. The most intriguing body feature, common to most of the black men present, was that their upper front tooth was missing. The white men wanted to know the purpose of the custom, but they didn't know how to ask. It was obviously an important tradition to the native men because they were keen to learn if the visitors had the same practice. George Worgan told his officer friends later:

'They thrust their fingers into our mouths to see if we'd parted with this tooth.'

By an amazing coincidence, Governor Phillip had exactly the same tooth missing in his mouth, and when the natives noticed this, George thought they were astonished and pleased. The white men later learnt that the tooth was removed as part of a ceremony when a native boy reached the stage of becoming a warrior. It explained the natives' surprise that the white leader had the same important feature.

Throughout their meeting, another important issue had been bothering the native men about the visitors.

What kind of creatures are the strangers?
Are they men or women?

It was impossible to tell by looking at them. Their bodies were completely covered. Their cheeks were smooth but they weren't behaving like women.

'Mula?' (Man) 'Gin?' (Woman) They used simple words to ask.

The visitors didn't understand their questions so the native men would have to wait for an answer to the baffling issue. However, the strangers carried weapons so for now, they treated the visitors as men.

****

When they returned to their ships, the white men felt positive about their meetings with the natives. Governor Phillip was happy with the progress they had made but he wasn't so pleased with Botany Bay itself. The area didn't provide a deep sheltered harbour for the ships, or a suitable place with enough running water for a settlement.

He decided to visit an unexplored bay to the north, marked on his map as 'Port Jackson'. On 21st January, he left Botany Bay to head north with a party of officers and some reliable convicts in three small boats to see what the unknown place offered.

In the meantime, he left officers, including Lieutenant Watkin Tench, to continue exploring Botany Bay. Doctor John White was also left at Botany Bay to check on the health of the convicts aboard the transport ships.

Chapter 9

21st January 1788, Botany Bay

Watkin Tench was a daring young marine who
had volunteered for a three-year tour of service
in the convict settlement in New South Wales.
For him the whole experience of the voyage
to an unknown land was an adventure.

His ship was one of the last to anchor in Botany Bay but he was
eager for a chance to go ashore. His party of men headed for the
south side of the harbour in a rowboat where they hoped to meet
some natives. He'd thought up a risky idea, thinking it would be the
perfect way to attract the natives' interest. He was taking a seven-
year-old boy ashore with him.

****

The natives stood in the shade that bordered the beach, watching
as a small boat drew closer to the water's edge. The people wading
ashore from the boat were a mystery. The only part of them visible
was their pale-coloured faces. The rest of their bodies were
completely hidden, even their feet and the tops of their heads were
covered. The native men were anxious about the visitors because
they'd already heard from others that they had strange ways.

As the white visitors walked slowly up the beach, the natives saw
that one of them was holding the hand of a little one.

The child's small, thin face was also as pale as sand. They stared in amazement.

The natives had their spears ready and the white men coming from the boats carried their muskets but the presence of a child had a calming effect. It seemed unlikely that weapons would be necessary. Watkin Tench wrote what happened in his journal.

The child seemed to attract their attention very much, for they frequently pointed to him and spoke to each other.

As they came closer and saw the whiteness of his skin they gave a loud exclamation, and one of the party, an old man, with a long beard came close to us.

The native with great gentleness, laid his hand on the child's hat and felt his clothes, muttering to himself all the while.

Other natives came forward for a closer look and to inspect the child's clothing. But by then the boy was becoming restless, and was taken back to the boat. Seeing this, the natives weren't offended. Tench noticed they'd kept their own children at a safe distance.

More white men then walked up the beach carrying a heavy object and from it they took out things which they offered to the natives.

'Mee diee?' (What are they?)

One of the natives put an object to his tongue but it was tasteless. It seemed a useless gift. Seeing he didn't understand the use of the object, one of the white men took the mirror from his hand and held it up to demonstrate that he should look into it.

'Look, you can see yourself,' the visitor said pointing to his reflection.

The native men didn't understand the words but got the meaning. But the object still seemed of no use when a pool of water served the same purpose.

Why would anyone bother carrying around such a thing?

Then the natives attempted to teach the visitors some basic words and though they repeated themselves patiently many times, the white men couldn't pronounce the words properly. After an hour, the natives gave up. The meeting was over and the visitors rowed back to their ship feeling positive about their meeting.

The natives however were still unsure of the newcomers' intentions. As they walked away, they wondered about the mysterious strangers; close up they were very unusual. Their noses were thin, their eyes pale, the odour of them was strange.

Who were the white beings?
Could they be spirits returned from death?

Chapter 10

January 1788, Botany Bay

While the Governor was away exploring the area to the north, some of the younger, stronger male convicts were ordered ashore under guard to cut wood for the ship's fires, collect grass for the animals aboard the ships and clear ground in case the Governor didn't find a better place to settle.

It was a huge effort for the men to use their aching limbs after months below deck in cramped conditions. The glare of the sun and the heat was unbearable. When they returned to the ships, the convicts below deck wanted to know about the animals, the reptiles and the natives.

'Did you see any cannibals?' The ship-bound convicts asked.

The workers had not seen any natives, but they had stories of very strange animals.

'We saw somethin' looks like a giant mouse, the size of a sheep, but it stands upright like a man.'

The convicts stared in amazement as the story continued.

'It has big hind feet and sits back on a long, thick tail.'

'But it don't run 'round fast like a mouse, does it?' a convict asked.

'Nay. It takes great leaps on its hind legs, pushing off with its tail. It moves mighty fast, that's for sure.'

'And we saw an even bigger creature, a huge bird! Stands taller than a man and can run much faster!'

'Is that the truth?' The ship-bound convicts were wide-eyed.

When the sailors and officers from *Lady Penrhyn* returned to the ship, the same fantastic stories spread to the women below deck. One of the men had even made a sketch of the creatures.

Elizabeth Hayward was extremely worried. She didn't want to show her fear but she wanted to ask more about the strange animals.

Were they fierce beasts? Would they attack her?

But she didn't say a word, she just looked at the drawings. Once they landed, she would have to go alone in the wilderness to the toilet at some stage. It was a frightening thought!

The officers and marines had their muskets for protection but how would she defend herself, if pounced on by a wild creature?

****

The convicts were all thinking about the day they would land. Some were scared about what they would have to face. Some were tired and depressed, dreading the work they would have to do, and some were just plain lazy. However, a few were eager to see what the strange new place would offer.

One convict, Thomas Barrett, the man who had made the fake coins during the voyage, was feeling rather pleased with himself. He suddenly had high hopes for his future because one of the doctors had given him an important and unusual job.

Doctor John White had not stopped thinking about the convict's incredible talent since he had seen the coins the young man had produced. So, while the ships were still anchored in Botany Bay, he saw an opportunity to put Thomas Barrett to work on a project using his artistic skills.

'Barrett, I want you to carve a medallion for me.'

'What would that be, sir?' The convict had no idea what 'medallion' meant.

'I want you to make a medal to commemorate the success of our voyage.' Doctor White explained.

'I don't understand com-em-o-rate, sir.'

'Commemorate means to remember something, Barrett. I want you to make a medal to remember and celebrate the success of our voyage.'

'Right you are then, Sir.' Barrett knew he didn't have a choice in the matter but engraving was better than any other job he could imagine.

The doctor handed him a metal bowl to carve the medal from, and a sketch of what he wanted on it.

'On one side, engrave an image of our ship *Charlotte* in Botany Bay. On the other side, put a description of our voyage. Here is a list for you to copy. Take care that you get it all in the space, lad.'

'As you say, Sir.' Barrett got to work creating the medal as ordered.

On the front, he etched an image of *Charlotte*. On the other side, he listed each port the fleet had called at, and the dates they'd stopped during the voyage.

As he worked, Thomas Barrett felt very satisfied with his situation. Other marines were already asking him to make things for them too. He felt sure he wouldn't be digging holes and chopping trees when the time came for landing and setting up camp. His talent, he believed, would lead to an easy life.

But that's not how things would turn out for Thomas Barrett.

---

* The Charlotte Medal is displayed at Australian National Maritime Museum, Sydney.

Chapter 11

January 1788, Botany Bay to Port Jackson

Meanwhile, Governor Phillip's party reached Port Jackson and sailed between the steep stone headlands, where they found a beautiful harbour.

This was much better than Botany Bay!

Phillip soon realised that the harbour was so extensive and offered so many possibilities they would have to camp overnight in order to explore it. News of the arrival of white men had travelled overland already because many natives came to meet them and receive gifts.

Next day, after more exploring, Phillip's group found what appeared to be a deserted cove on the south side of Port Jackson. They were pleased to find it had a fresh water stream and an area perfect for a settlement. Phillip was impressed with the little bay where ships could anchor close to the shore, and at a small expense wharves could be built for unloading supplies.

Without thinking that the little cove had already been given a name by the people who lived there, Phillip proudly declared:

'We will call the place Sydney Cove.'

Governor Phillip returned to Botany Bay with his party, to announce their magnificent find and to order an immediate transfer of the whole fleet northward to Sydney Cove.

****

The native clans living around the bay they called *Kamay* (Botany Bay) watched the white strangers pack up and leave their territory.

When they'd arrived days earlier, the ghostly pale people had come ashore in their bizarre body coverings, speaking a strange language, and looking as if they may stay for a while. They had cut down trees, dug holes and hunted animals. Then suddenly they had decided to move on, and the black families were relieved.

The uninvited strangers had seemed friendly at first, offering their unusual gifts, but their ways were so very different. The natives who had met with them would send messages northward, to those related to them through marriage, warning the *Cadigal* and *Wangal* clans that they may receive a visit from a large number of strange white beings.

Chapter 12

January 1788, Sydney Cove (Warran)

In the quiet bay they called *'Warran'*, natives watched from a safe distance as the biggest *nowee* they'd ever seen entered the little cove. Soon after, a smaller boat was lowered over its side, bringing the white men close enough to wade ashore.

Now, one of the white strangers splashed towards the bank carrying another man on his back. The one being carried wore a bright red coat, which the natives had already learnt, meant he was important. As the men reached the water's edge, the man in the red jacket jumped into the shallow water and lost his balance. As he stumbled and splashed about, his hat floated across the water out of reach. The other white men laughed and cheered, and the natives hidden within the trees around the cove couldn't help smiling to themselves.

Maybe the strangers are not so strange after all.
Perhaps they are just young men like us having fun.

The black men could not have known that the laughter between the groups of white men *was* strange, very strange indeed. It was unusual because the two men coming ashore were at opposite ends of a great social divide. One man was a prisoner, James Ruse, convicted for theft. The man on his back was Lieutenant George Johnston of the British marines.

The native men watching could not know that the white men were from a distant country where people were divided by levels of importance.

People in Britain belonged to either the upper class, or the lower class, and the levels were not easily crossed. The higher classes of British society believed in keeping the lower classes powerless. A group known as 'the criminal class', had no rights at all.

The laughter the natives had watched would not be likely in Britain. But in this quiet cove, far away from Britain, the joking was a sign that already things were beginning to change for the convicts. Lieutenant Johnston, the cause of the amusement, had sensed it too, but it hadn't worried him. In fact, it would suit him because he was falling in love with a convict named Esther Abraham.

As he walked up the slope of the thickly wooded cove feeling his legs adapt to solid ground, he thought about Esther, the convict he would take as his housekeeper. She wasn't rough like some of the other women. In fact, she was lovely. He pictured her long black hair, her almond shaped eyes and slender face.

It had been a difficult voyage for her, trying to look after her baby daughter who'd been born in prison before the ships sailed from England. It wasn't easy, keeping a baby healthy in the conditions on the ship, but she was devoted to her little daughter.

George Johnston reflected on the story of her crime and conviction: Esther had been accused of stealing a roll of black lace from a store in London and had been lucky to escape death by hanging. She was nineteen at the time of her court case and swore she was innocent. She said the roll of lace had fallen to the ground from the counter as she walked by, but another customer said the roll had dropped from beneath Esther's coat as she tried to leave the store with it hidden.

She received a sentence of transportation to Botany Bay, sailing on *Lady Penrhyn*, under the supervision of Lieutenant Johnston.

Well, he'd look after them both, Esther and her daughter, from now on. When they came ashore, he'd give them the protection his position as an officer allowed. He would provide a little hut for them to live in as soon as it was possible.

'Lieutenant Johnston!'

The sound of his name brought him back to reality. The tall, fair-haired young Scotsman squared his broad shoulders and braced himself for the task ahead. There was so much work to do!

****

Before the main fleet arrived in Sydney Cove, Governor Phillip had already begun preparation for the site. A priority was to claim the territory for Britain and he recorded the event in his journal:

> *In the evening of the 26th, the flag was displayed on shore, and the Governor, with several of his officers and others, assembled round the flag-staff, and drank the king's health and success to the settlement.*

Phillip knew the convict settlement at Sydney Cove could be no ordinary prison with the usual high stone walls and metal bars to keep the criminals locked away. He would use chains on prisoners if necessary, and public floggings to keep control. As a last resort, he would order executions by public hanging. He would have to show from the start that he would not deal lightly with law-breakers.

He hoped fear of the unknown would stop the convicts from thinking about escaping from the settlement. Already many of them seemed afraid of the forest that reached almost to the water's edge. But he needed to know in advance which convicts were trustworthy and which of them would have to be closely watched.

With all the ships anchored in Sydney Cove, the Governor consulted his officers aboard the different ships about the conduct of convicts during the voyage.

****

Painting by Frank Allen

James Ruse, the convict who had carried Lieutenant Johnston ashore, stood on the edge of the forest with the officers, marines and male convicts, gazing around the peaceful little bay the Governor had just named 'Sydney Cove'. It was wild and unfamiliar.

A fresh-water stream flowed silently through a forest of tall, majestic trees. Sunlight filtered through, lighting up the carpet of ferns edging the water. The scene had a calm, soothing effect which they all knew was about to be shattered by the sounds of hammers and axes. The quiet little cove would never be the same again.

Ruse felt a sense of anticipation he had not expected about this new place. He had behaved well during the voyage and it had already paid off because he'd been chosen for the first landing party. The laughter caused by the lieutenant's tumble into the water had made him feel optimistic about his future. As he looked around, he could see that men with farming experience like him would be necessary.

****

Painting by Ian Hansen

Ruse wondered about little John Hudson. He had met the young chimneysweep while on the prison hulk *Dunkirk* before they'd been put aboard different First Fleet ships. He hoped the boy had survived the voyage. He decided he would look out for him once all the convicts were landed and take an interest in him. The poor boy had no one else.

***

While the clearing work was underway, the female convicts and children were kept on the ships until tents were set up for them. As they waited to step onto land for the first time in almost a year, some were feeling uneasy about their new surroundings.

Elizabeth Hayward leaned on the ship's rail, taking in the strangeness of the place. The air was hot and humid. Unfamiliar smells tickled her nostrils; a sweet peppery aroma wafted from the woodland.

Looking to the shoreline, she saw the mish mash of tents dotting the clearing amid fallen trees, boxes, piles of provisions and equipment. Marines in their red jackets and black hats paraded around the place trying to look busy, as groups of male convicts were bullied and pressed to carry boxes or drag logs.

How could they work in the stifling heat?

Her thoughts were interrupted by a weird cackling noise coming from somewhere among the trees. The strange chortling sound increased to a chorus of wild laughter. It was as if hidden creatures were mocking the workers from within the forest.

Haha, Hoohoo, Kaka, kookoo haha

The men working ashore stopped and looked around, puzzled.

Someone pointed to a line of plump birds perched high on a branch warbling out the most outlandish sounds the visitors had ever heard. The birdcall was so like wild laughter that someone suggested calling them 'laughing jackasses'. No sooner had the cackling faded away, leaving the newcomers to continue their unpacking, when a series of high-pitched, blood-curdling screeches broke the silence. This time the shrieks had come from a large white bird swooping low across the clearing. The place was filled with unexpected sights and sounds.

Old Dorothy Handland shuffled up to Elizabeth.

'We're in the middle o' nowhere amid who knows what, lass.
How will I ever survive this God-forsaken place?'

Elizabeth shrugged, knowing Dorothy would not wait for an answer.

'But survive it I must, coz I'm heading back to old England when me time's done.'

Elizabeth just nodded. Dorothy repeated the same thing every day. As the old woman chatted on, Elizabeth was aware of a whirring noise in the background. The sound had gradually increased to a deafening buzz. Then it had suddenly stopped for a minute, before starting up again. She looked around to see if anyone else noticed it.

'Cicadas, lass.' A seamen working nearby yelled above the noise.
'They 'ave 'em in China too. Just annoyin' insects.'

Elizabeth had no idea where China was, but she wanted to ask,
'Do they attack people? Do they bite or sting?'

Instead she gazed toward the grey-green forest. Even with all the strange sounds coming from it, it was very still.

****

Esther Abrahams had heard the sounds too as she stood nursing her baby girl, Rosanna. She was from the lively, bustling city of London.

She wasn't used to wild, eerie, empty places. She looked to the forest, wondering what was lurking there, looking for signs of movement. She thought of the rumours that had spread during the voyage.

She'd heard the stories of giant snakes and spiders, but she was an intelligent woman and would put those ideas out of her head.

How would any of them know what's there?
No one had ventured far into the forest yet.

Esther held her baby daughter closer. They had already been through so much. Newgate prison had been terrible. The voyage had been frightening, exhausting, and at times she thought it would never end. But all that was behind them at last.

Now that they were anchored safely in the small cove, they were facing another challenge. Uncertainty lay ahead as they prepared to leave the ship and live in tents in this unknown land. In the scene before Esther, there was not a single familiar sight. No roads, no fences, no buildings...just wilderness.

****

Esther's attention was brought back to the deck of the *Lady Penrhyn* as shouting filled the air. She watched as Ann Smith, a convict in her early thirties, put on another of her frequent outbursts.

'You can keep your slops. I won't be needing 'em!' Ann yelled as she threw the bundle of clothes onto the deck. 'I won't be stayin' round long enough to need 'em .'

The other women exchanged glances. Mr Miller, the man in charge of the stores, had just come on board to hand out clothing, known as 'slops', in preparation for the women going ashore after tents had been erected.

Mr Miller glanced at the pile of rough clothing lying on the deck and glared back at the woman. If they weren't so busy with everything else this women would definitely receive a flogging. She'd behaved badly all through the voyage, constantly announcing she'd escape.

'Oh well, let her try,' he thought. 'She doesn't deserve the clothes. We're short of supplies and we've no idea when more will arrive.'

The convicts watching Ann's outburst also remembered her constant talk of escape, and they began to suspect that she may actually do it. When she'd boasted of it during the voyage, the other women had thought it was all nonsense but now, it seemed she was serious.

Where on earth would she go?
How would she live out there in the wild?

****

As the doling out of clothing continued, Ann Smith looked to the shore and took in the scenery. She had already weighed up her options and she could see her daring plan taking shape. She knew how and when she would do it.

****

Across the bay aboard *Charlotte*, Susannah balanced her little son on her hip. She was nervous about landing but she was excited too. She'd been separated from Henry, her baby's father, for months and soon they would be together again. She gazed at the peaceful forest and felt a wave of hope as she took in her surroundings.

The shrieking birds had startled her at first, but when she realised what they were, the birdcalls had represented freedom.

Speckled shafts of sunlight fell between the trees, lighting the forest floor. The scene was one of wild beauty. The sky however, had the greatest impact on her senses. It's brightness dazzled her, filling her with uplifting thoughts.

After years in prison, then the voyage, this strange place held promise. After the landing of all the convicts, she'd marry Henry Kable as they'd promised to do. The Governor was encouraging marriage here. She felt sure her life would be better from now on.

She thought back to the time, almost a year before, when they had taken her baby from her. Things had become so unbearable that she hadn't wanted to live and had thought of ending her life. She was glad she hadn't had the opportunity to go through with her threat. She breathed in the fresh air.

There's no filth. There are no slums.
There's space...This could be a new start for our little family.

****

The convicts weren't the only ones forming opinions. The officers and marines also had mixed reactions to their new surroundings. Lieutenant Ralph Clark, who had volunteered for service in the colony, had been very positive as he sailed toward the little cove, named Sydney.

'I never saw anything like it! It's the most beautiful place.' Clark declared over and over. 'I am quite charmed with the place.'

Watching from the ship as tents went up around the shoreline, he thought the scene was very picturesque. But two days later his opinion changed when it was his turn to go ashore and pitch his tent amid the trees. Sleeping on the ground near the edge of the forest, as a storm raged, he saw things very differently.

He was feeling very sorry for himself when he wrote in his journal:

What a terrible night it was last night with thunder, lightning and rain. I was obliged to get out of my tent with nothing on but my shirt to fix the tent poles... It's remarkably hot here!

I have nothing to sleep in but a poor tent and a little grass to lie on.

Within days of setting up camp, Lieutenant Clark was regretting he had volunteered for his 'tour of duty' in New South Wales. He was wishing he had never set foot in the place as he told his wife, Betsy, in a letter to her in England:

My God, the thunder and lightning here is incredible! I was very much frightened. Above all the places in the world, this is the most terrible for thunder and lightning.

In all the course of my life, I never slept worse my dear wife, than I did last night - what with the hard cold ground, spiders, ants and every awful thing that you can think of, crawling over me, I was glad when the morning came.

I could not stay in this place longer than three years for the world. I wish I could get home now.

And so, with such a mixed collection of people, each with their own plans, personalities and attitudes, Governor Phillip had to build a colony. The adventure, toil and mystery of a new world had begun.

Part 2

Life at Sydney Cove

Painting by Ian Hansen

Chapter 13

Sydney Cove, February 1788

By the end of January, the work of clearing the area for storehouses, tents and other buildings was well underway but it had been an enormous job.

Tall trees had covered the area and the removal of them had been more difficult than they'd expected. The men soon found that the timber of the enormous trees was extremely hard. When they swung their axes at them, they just bounced off. When they tried to push their spades into the ground, the surface was rock hard. Axe handles were breaking; spades and saw blades became blunt.

The convicts' backs were suffering badly. They'd been cooped up on a ship for nearly a year, some had been in prison much longer. Their muscles were scrawny, their legs feeble, their arms weak. They cursed the stony ground and the blazing sun that burnt and blistered their skin. They weren't used to the stifling heat and humidity but the back-breaking clearing work had to be done as quickly as possible. The Governor's secretary described the scene:

> *Parties of people were everywhere seen and heard doing various jobs. Some clearing ground for the different camps, others pitching tents, or carrying stores…and the spot, which had recently been a place of peace and silence, had changed to one of noise and confusion.*

****

Native eyes watched the campsite from the high ground around the cove with a mixture of shock, alarm and amazement. They were very puzzled.

Why are they cutting trees down? And why so many?

Don't they know it will affect the hunting, and shade will be lost for the herbs and ferns?

Don't they understand trees are needed to make canoes and shields?

They'd been mystified to watch men struggle for hours to bring down a tall, straight, slender tree, remove all its branches, drag it across the clearing and after digging a hole, plant it again.

Why were the strangers, huffing and puffing in the heat to move trees from one place to another?

What was the point? Was it part of a ritual?

Then they watched as a piece of the same stuff they used to cover their bodies, was attached to the tree and hoisted to the top. Men had then stood around it, looking up and shouting the strange words: 'Health...Majesty...Colony'.

There appeared to be divisions between the white people too. Some were being forced to work by others who struck them. Some had come ashore tied together while others shouted words at them.

'Hurry! Get moving!'

The natives looked on, feeling perplexed. They would keep watch from a distance. In the meantime, they decided, it was a place for them and their children to avoid. The question most on their mind was,

'How long will the strangers stay?'

****

Governor Phillip walked around giving orders and inspecting the progress. His plan for the settlement had already been drawn.

His headquarters had been set up in a marquee, or large canvas tent, on the east side of the cove. Nearby storehouses, vegetable gardens and a blacksmith's shop were underway. Tents for well-behaved convicts, who'd be his household servants, were set up near his headquarters. Behind that, an area for a government farm was being cleared and dug.

On the western point of the cove, an observatory was being built under the direction of Lieutenant Dawes, who was to observe the stars with equipment brought from England. Also on the western side, the marine camp and their parade ground, a portable canvas hospital and the main area of convicts' tents was in progress. A freshwater stream ran between the two areas.

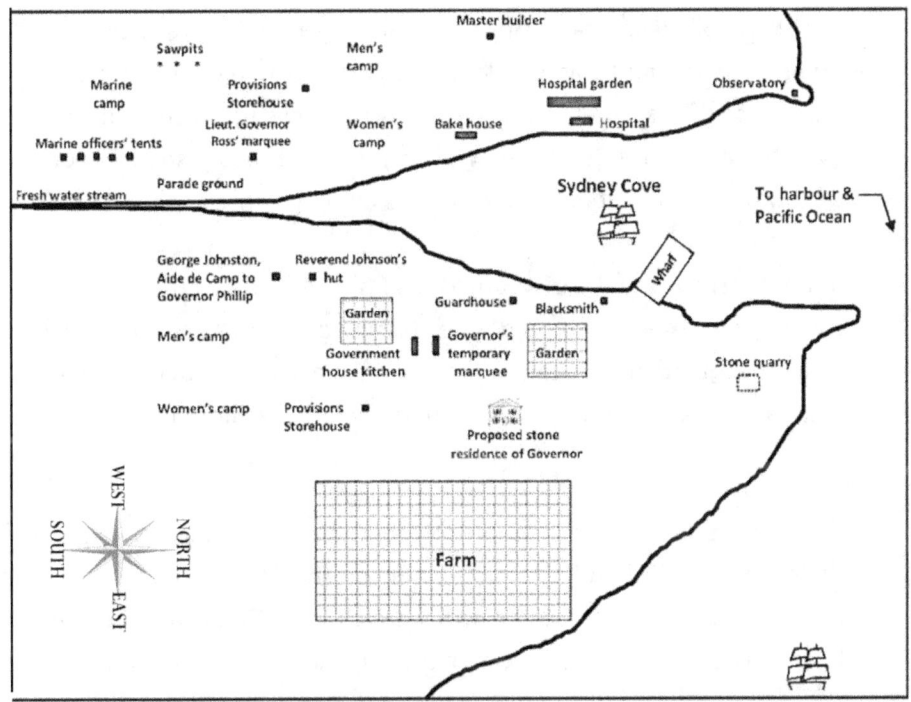

Gradually a settlement was taking shape despite the poor tools and a lack of skilled labour. The area that once sat quietly beside the bay, its stream flowing through a tranquil forest for thousands of years, had now become a hubbub of noisy activity.

****

By late afternoon on 6th February all the female convicts and children were finally landed. It became a lively night as friends and couples were reunited. Henry and Susannah were in each other's arms again after so long apart, and happily planning their wedding day.

An intense storm hit the cove on the same night bringing heavy rain and fierce lightning that battered the tents and split trees, killing some pigs and sheep enclosed in pens. The damage and confusion left the campsite and its inhabitants looking quite a mess.

But the following day, Governor Phillip established discipline, ordering everyone to assemble in the clearing. It was time for the reading of official orders prepared in Britain, giving instructions on everything to do with the new government. It was also time for Governor Phillip to address the convicts directly and set some rules.

It was a showy and noisy affair. The soldiers marched into the clearing with their drums and flutes blaring out military music. They formed a guard round the gathering of convict men and women who sat in a large group on the ground; there were more than seven hundred of them.

The officers and marines stood to attention in full military dress, their rows of polished buttons gleaming on their bright red woollen jackets. The Governor waited for the crowd to be hushed before taking his position before them; his smart blue jacket signifying his position in the Royal Navy. A table was set up before the crowd and two red leather cases, containing the official instructions, were opened and read with a show of great importance.

The official talk went over the heads of most of the convicts but then the Governor addressed them directly. He surveyed the gathering before him and in a firm voice, he told them:

'I will show encouragement and favour to those of you who obey orders and show good conduct,' the Governor said, then paused.

'On the other hand, those who act badly will certainly meet with the punishment they deserve. Any act of cruelty to the natives is forbidden and make no mistake, stealing will be punished by death.'

After his address, the military band played 'God Save the King' while parading around the camp, officers received salutes and three volleys were fired into the air by the troops to mark the importance of the occasion.

****

The native inhabitants of the area, unable to ignore the loud, colourful activity in the visitors' camp, were more baffled than ever by what was happening there. They decided they would send scouts into the strangers' camp to see, and try to understand, what was going on.

****

As the soldiers marched off and the convicts were ordered back to their various jobs, some forgot about the Governor's speech immediately. Others continued to think about his words.

James Ruse, the convict who had carried Lieutenant Johnston ashore two weeks earlier, had paid special attention to the Governor's offer of encouragement for good conduct. He believed he understood the Governor's deeper meaning.

'The Gov'nor is actually offering an *incentive* to those who behave well,' he said to young John Hudson who was working beside him.

'What's in-cen-tive?' John Hudson asked, only half listening.

'It's like a reward to get people to do something,' Ruse explained, hoping to raise the lad's curiosity. 'Someone offers an incentive when they really need other people to do something.'

But he could see young John wasn't interested. He didn't have vision.

'I just want to stay out of trouble, that's all.' John muttered.

Unfortunately, the lad was like so many around him with no energy or drive. Ruse was used to seeing the disinterested expressions on the faces of convicts he worked with, and knew he was different. The Governor needed men with motivation and get-up-and-go, and James Ruse knew he had it.

However he would wait for the right time before approaching the Governor with a plan. It wouldn't be too long before his seven-year sentence was over. He would wait till then.

****

Another convict was thinking the same thing but with a very different attitude and a much more daring plan. Ann Smith, the convict who planned to escape, hadn't had a chance to do so during the Governor's speech because they were surrounded by guards the whole time. But there would be other events happening soon when everyone would be distracted. She would make her move then...

****

The day after the Governor's address, two native elders visited the settlement to investigate the goings-on of the foreigners' camp.

Entering the place of the strangers was a mission of great courage for the scouts. But the white leader, the one with the missing tooth, welcomed them with seeming pride at the changes he and his people had brought to the place. He pointed to the different shelters they had put up, saying words like 'storehouse' and to another place with a fire burning before it, he said 'blacksmith'. The elders nodded.

The white leader offered some spongy white matter he called 'bread' and a portion of dried meat he called 'pork', But the black men were wary of its strange smell. They tasted it but didn't want to swallow it. The leader, who was called 'Gov-er-nor', gave them some coloured water he called 'wine'. It hurt their throats. They would not taste it a second time.

All the white men and women were still wrapped in their strange body coverings even with the heat of summer. By then, the natives had worked out that the men and women wore different coverings. That was how they knew which was which. Some of the men were in the bright red body coverings that the natives already knew meant they had power. They carried the *gooroobeera* [4] *(fire stick weapons)* that the black men had seen at work in the forest. They had watched the weapons kill animals at a great distance, and they knew to avoid the ones who carried them.

The elders returned from the white settlement to their people unharmed, with gifts of hatchets and an account of all the mysterious things they'd seen. They described the structures where some of the strangers lay sick and dying. Another area of the camp seemed to be for the use of the 'redcoats' only. There, on a trodden, dusty plot of ground, they carried on strange rituals. Amid calls and commands they marched with their weapons to their shoulders. The scene was perplexing.

****

[4] 'Gooroobeera' was the word used by Aboriginal people to mean white men's guns.

In a nearby cove, eight-year-old Nanberry lived with his family and relatives. Like all the native children there, he'd heard discussions among his people about the baffling things that happened in the new settlement. Around the campfire, they'd been warned again by the elders to avoid the place. He was curious but he would respect and obey them. He would stay away from the strangers' site.

****

The Governor was very pleased with the visit from the natives. After the elders left the camp, his secretary wrote about their stay.

Two men strolled into the camp this afternoon, and stayed for about an hour. They appeared to admire whatever they saw, and after receiving a hatchet each they left, apparently pleased with their reception.

Encouraged by the occasion, Governor Phillip addressed his officers. 'We must do everything we can to continue this friendly contact.'

While he had their attention, he mentioned another issue that had come to his notice.

'I must announce again to everyone – convicts, marines and sailors – that taking the spears, fishing gear and tools of the natives is strictly forbidden.' He spoke in a meaningful tone.

'They leave their equipment around the rocks and on the beaches unprotected as it seems they are honest among themselves. But I have reason to suspect some of the boat crew have stolen their tools to sell as souvenirs in Europe. It must be stopped!'

'The loss of their tools must cause great problems for the owners, as it is obviously their primary way of getting their food,' he said. 'Some of the convicts are also beginning to go wandering about collecting native equipment to sell to the seamen. They must be more closely guarded and know they will be severely punished.'

The officers agreed. But they knew it was not easy keeping all the convicts restricted to the settlement. The surrounding forest was becoming less frightening than it had been at first to some of them.

****

February 10th 1788 was a very special day for Henry and Susannah Kable. It was an occasion they had been looking forward to for years. They stood proudly before the Reverend Richard Johnson, who conducted their wedding service beneath a shady tree by the harbour. Before a gathering of convicts they promised their lives to each other and then signed their names in the register with an X, as neither of them could write.

Since his arrival at Sydney Cove, Henry Kable had gained the Governor's trust. He'd proved he was a level-headed young man, devoted to his partner and child. So the couple went to live near the Governor's canvas residence on the eastern side of the cove. There a select group of reliable male and female convicts worked as his household servants and as supervisors over the government farm being planted. Henry was to be overseer of the women's camp.

As they put their few possessions into their tent, the young couple smiled at each other.

'Oh Henry, I could never 'ave imagined a time like this. Together as a family, with our little boy!' Susannah hugged her son, who by now was an energetic toddler who everyone called Young Harry.

'It's only a tent for now, my love. But as soon as I can, I'll build us a little hut. And when we finally get those things we were given by the kind people of London, we'll be doing alright.'

'Yes,' Susannah smiled. 'And we're doing alright now I think Henry. I'll make us some Johnny-cakes to celebrate.'

She quickly mixed some of their ration of flour with water. Then balancing the metal end of their shovel on a rock in the open fire, she fried the flattened dough in fat until it began to sizzle.

As they sat watching the cakes become crisp, Henry again raised the subject of the crate of donated goods that had been loaded onto a ship for their use once in the colony.

'It's worryin' me,' he said, 'that each time I ask about the things, it's brushed aside. I'll try asking about it again tomorrow.'

Just then, something small and shiny dropped into Susannah's lap and she jumped up, screaming.

'It's just a beetle of some sort, lass. It's gone now. We have to get used to such things.' Henry said gently.

'I know, I know,' Susannah snapped. 'It's just that everything is so strange here. I'll get used to it all one day.'

They were both very aware how many aspects of life in Sydney Cove were different to England. For Susannah, the insects and animals were scary and the violent thunderstorms were alarming.

For Henry, the soil was disappointing but he would try growing potatoes and cabbage to add to their allowance of rice, flour and salt-pork. They had also gathered wild greens in the forest, like spinach and parsley.

There was a vine growing in the area that some of the convicts brewed into a sweet tea and some sour red berries they could stew into jam. There was fish too. They would be alright.

Bringing his attention back to their new set up, Henry said cheerily, 'I'll try making us a table and chairs when I get spare time.'

****

Meanwhile, in mid-February, as timber storehouses and vegetable gardens began appearing in Sydney Cove, the Governor sent one of his officers on a very important mission. Lieutenant King was to establish another British settlement on a tiny island, way out in the Pacific Ocean, to prevent any other European country occupying it. Another reason for going to Norfolk Island was to cultivate a plant called *flax* that was valuable for making strong fabric for ships' sails.

Lieutenant King was taking a small party of twenty-two people, including a doctor, a handful of marines and a group of fifteen convicts. It was a difficult assignment for a young officer because there were few places on earth as isolated as the island he was to settle and very little was known about it.

The day of the departure of the little group heading to Norfolk Island was distressing for Elizabeth Hayward because the women chosen to go there had been with her on the *Lady Penrhyn*. During the voyage, and since arriving in Sydney Cove, they had treated Elizabeth like their little sister. She felt miserable as she watched them sail away. They had shared their secrets, their joys and sorrows in the overcrowded quarters of *Lady Penrhyn* for those long trying months of the voyage. No one knew when, or if, they would ever meet again.

****

While almost everyone in the settlement was busy saying goodbye to their friends leaving for Norfolk Island, Ann Smith, the convict who had declared she would escape, took the opportunity to quietly sneak out of the Sydney campsite.

Once her disappearance became know, the women who'd listened to her crazy ideas during the voyage, were astounded that she had actually gone through with her plan. They were stunned that she would attempt life alone in the mysterious wilderness.

What would become of her?

Even in the safety of the settlement, the convicts were still checking over their shoulders for the scary creatures they believed were lurking in the forest, afraid that one day they may meet face to face.

****

A few days later something happened to make everyone more cautious about the dangers of wandering too far from the settlement. During the morning, someone came staggering into camp as white as a sheet after making a toilet visit.

'An alligator – in the bu-bushes – near the edge of camp.'
The man stuttered. 'It was huge! It was near the stream.'

Feeling more confident within a circle of curious men, he led them back to the area, but there was nothing there.

'It was eight feet long[5], I tell you. As long as a rowboat, I swear it.'

[5] eight feet = 2.4 metres

Some time later, news flashed around the settlement that a sailor had gone missing. He was last seen just before dark, standing near the edge of the camp. Then he had vanished into thin air.

It wasn't long before another sighting was reported near the tents. This time the alligator was reported to be fourteen feet long[6].

Doctor John White, a keen and knowledgeable scientist, questioned the people who reported seeing the terrifying creature.

'Did the reptile attack you?'

'No, it stayed still, but I didn't wait around for it to catch me. When I did look back, it had gone up a tree.'

'Well,' said Doctor White, always keen to give his opinion. 'I doubt very much it was an alligator. I think what you saw was some type of large lizard. They won't hurt you.'

But the women in particular were still worried and went to the toilet in groups and kept a lookout for one another.

That sensational episode no sooner died down than a group of convicts reported seeing a tiger one evening, hiding in the bushes, not far from the tents.

'Oh, it's just another crazy creation of their wild imagination.' Doctor White told the Governor, then he added in a mocking tone, 'But you know, when a man is scared out of his wits, a bush in the dark might easily be mistaken for a tiger.'

'Or they may have seen one of the wild dogs the natives call *dingo*,' another officer suggested. 'They seem pretty harmless though. In fact, the natives keep them as pets.'

The Governor was thoughtful. There was still the business of the missing sailor.

****

[6] fourteen feet = 4.2 metres

A week after the sailor disappeared, he was found in the forest near Botany Bay, two hours' walk from the camp. He had wandered into the wilderness and lost his way. When his rescuers found him, he was half-starved and terrified. He said that in the whole time he'd been gone, he had eaten only a handful of shellfish he'd picked from the rocks. He said the natives had chased him, taken his clothes and pelted him with stones. He'd been so afraid that he'd waded into a swamp where he'd hidden neck-deep in water among the reeds until hunger had forced him to keep walking in search of food and the campsite.

'Well, at least your return to camp has ended talk of death by alligator or death by tiger,' Doctor White joked as he dressed his wounds. But the sailor did not think his ordeal was funny.

Soon afterward, the people of Sydney Cove learnt that large intimidating creatures did exist in the area not far from their camp. Two incidents happened on the same day and this time the reporters had the evidence to prove it.

The first sighting was when some sailors from *Lady Penrhyn* went searching for herbs in the forest. One of them had just walked into some reeds near a swampy place when he gave a sudden shriek.

'What's that? I nearly stood on it!' he yelled, leaping from the spot.

It was a very large snake, bigger than any of them had ever seen and they wasted no time in shooting it.

John Hudson was among the crowd that gathered to see the huge dead reptile when it was brought in to Sydney Cove. He stared wide-eyed as he put out his hand to feel its scales. He couldn't wait to describe it to those who'd missed out on the show.

'It was as thick as a man's arm and over eight feet long, with a

eight feet = 2.4 metres

wide mouth with two rows of sharp pointed teeth...but only two big ones in its lower jaw.' He blurted excitedly, repeating the words exactly as he'd heard them. 'It was a very dark colour, almost black, with bright yellow spots along its whole length.'

'Well you'd best check where you step when you're in swampy ground collectin' reeds 'n rushes.' James Ruse reminded him.

In the excitement, John had forgotten that he was to start work with a group of rush-cutters, going down the harbour by boat to cut bunches of reeds and rushes for roof coverings. Now he wasn't keen on the idea, but it wasn't for him to pick and choose his work.

'I hear somethin' else pretty big was caught today in the harbour. Seein' our work's done, shall we go take a look, lad?' Ruse asked.

So they headed down to the water's edge where they saw an enormous shark, caught earlier in the day by the crew of *Sirius*. Its mouth, when fully open, was wide enough to swallow John's skinny body whole.

'Makes you think twice about going in the water, don't it lad.'

John Hudson looked across the bay to where native canoes dipped and bobbed on the waves. They were skillful people, the way they paddled so confidently in their lightly built craft...and they were fearless the way they sat balanced scarcely above the water.

****

From the high ground, the native families watched wide-eyed as the white men carried felled trees and laid them over a frame to form a track that led into the water. Along this pathway they carried boxes and rolled barrels between their boats and the shore.

Ian Hansen

The four-footed creatures brought from the boats onto land were very strange. The animals made the most peculiar bleating, bellowing and oinking sounds that had ever pierced the little cove. They were alien undreamed-of looking beasts. Some were short, stocky animals with stiff, squiggly tails, flattened snouts with big nostrils. They were covered with an almost hairless skin of the same shade as the men who herded them ashore.

There were other short animals with even weirder body coverings. They had a thick layer of something that the natives had never seen before and made sad bleating sounds, like a chorus of crying children.

There were also much bigger fearsome looking beasts, larger than any animal the black men had ever imagined, each with two pointed bones coming from its head. These worrying creatures stamped their feet and made loud menacing mooing sounds.

****

Over the weeks, the natives observed the way of living in the new settlement and it had shown them that the white boat people were indeed very different. After another passage of the moon, they suspected that they were not just passing through. They had stripped the little cove of trees and littered the place with their strange equipment. At first they'd been curious about the newcomers' unusual shelters, their cooking pots, the cutting and hammering tools, and the unfamiliar animals of all shapes and sizes. But the novelty had worn off.

From their canoes, they witnessed the damage to the site that had once given shade and provided food. The trees, where birds and honeybees had once lived, were now only ugly stumps. The sweet fragrant bushes that blossomed with fluffy golden clusters of sugar treats were already disappearing around the settlement.

Where was their respect for the land?

But that wasn't all the natives had observed about the settlement. From a distance, they had several times witnessed men stripped to the waist, tied to a specially made frame and beaten continuously with something designed to cause great pain. The whipping device was made from stiff animal skins of many cords, with hard knots along its length. All the while, as the flogging continued, the victims could not move.

The lashing went on long after deep, bloody gashes crisscrossed the white flesh. Seeing this, the black men had turned away, not because they were afraid of the sight of blood, but because it didn't seem fair to them. Their warrior code held that someone accused of a crime must face their accusers and defend their body.

However, much worse things happened in the strangers' camp. One summer afternoon just before sunset, the natives were drawn to the Sydney settlement by the sound of drums. From the high ground, they saw all the white people gathered in the clearing. They looked fearful, their heads were bowed, no one spoke. The redcoats had marched to the clearing carrying their weapons and surrounded the whole group. The natives looked on in astonishment as a young man was led trembling to a tree where a platform had been built. A rope hung from the tree.

The young person was prodded to climb what they later learnt was a 'ladder' and there the rope was pulled over his head. Standing rigid and armed with their weapons, the redcoats didn't move. A man covered in black from head to foot spoke a few words to the young man but no-one came forward to stop his suffering as he stood quivering and helpless. They all just stared, silently.

And later, after the hanging, when the body dangled limply, they had just lowered their heads, turned and slowly walked away. It was a disturbing sight for the observers.

****

The native people didn't know that the executed man was a talented metal engraver by the name of Thomas Barrett. They didn't understand that he'd been executed for stealing food from the public store on the very day that he received his share with all the other convicts.

****

Governor Phillip was also disturbed by Thomas Barrett's execution. It was the first hanging he'd ordered in Sydney Cove. But he'd had to make an example of the young offender. He'd tried to be fair in providing exactly the same food rations to the convicts as to the soldiers and officers, but the man Barrett had been greedy.

In their isolated situation, they had no idea when more supplies would arrive. He couldn't show weakness when it came to punishing people who stole food. However, that didn't make the man's death any less troubling. Phillip hoped it would send a message to the rest of the convicts. He had made it compulsory for them all to attend.

****

John Hudson and Elizabeth Hayward, now both fourteen, had stood among the crowd watching the execution and had similar reactions. They decided they must stay out of trouble.

Elizabeth learnt that she was to become a servant to Reverend Johnson, the man dressed in black who prayed with Thomas Barrett before his death. Old Dorothy thought it amusing to give her advice.

'You'll 'ave to watch your manners then, lass,' she joked, knowing the girl made smart comments sometimes.

Elizabeth Hayward wondered how life would change for her when she went to live in the household of Reverend Johnson and his quiet wife.

Chapter 14

Sydney Cove, March 1788

Despite the setbacks and troublemakers, Governor Phillip was feeling positive about the settlement and hopeful for its future. He had just inspected the work at Lieutenant Dawes' observatory on the western point of the cove. Movable panels were set into the cone-shaped roof so he could observe the stars at night. The plan was going well.

Returning to the camp along the high path around the bay, Phillip had a view of the settlement and could see progress. He couldn't help admiring it.

The first white settlement in the great south land!
Order will be brought to the wilderness.

Something however had been bothering him. With all the activity in the area and the immense changes brought to the place, he couldn't understand why the native people weren't showing more interest.

He could sense them watching the settlement, from the ridges and from their canoes but they wouldn't come into it.

What was keeping them away?

When he discussed the issue with his officers they assured him that, out on the harbour, contact between the black and white men had been co-operative.

'When the fishing nets are hauling in big catches, the native men assist willingly, and in return they receive a share of the fish.' Doctor White, a keen fisherman, assured him.

'Yes, and when our people are collecting oysters on the rocks around the headlands, the natives are friendly if we meet any. Or when we've been in the forest looking for edible greens, they seem pleased to show us which plants are suitable,' he added.

'Yes but they refuse any invitation to come into the settlement,' replied the Governor irritably.

'Well, there was the visit from the two old men a few weeks back Sir. They seemed pleased with everything they saw.' Watkin Tench reminded him.

'But no-one has returned for another look. In fact the opposite has happened, they seemed to be avoiding the place.'

Governor Phillip was growing impatient. His instructions from England had been to build an agreeable relationship with the natives. He wanted to know how *they* lived and had hoped to exchange information. He wanted to learn about the surrounding district and hoped they would act as guides.

Couldn't they see the advantages the British could offer them?
Couldn't they see the superior way of life in the settlement?

He would have to work on a plan to get some of them into the settlement. Once they saw all the benefits first hand, others would follow he was sure.

****

The natives, as they paddled past, had observed the massive changes brought to the area. They'd seen the large spaces opened up in the forest, the strange structure going up on the western point of the cove and the gradual flattening of ferns. They'd discussed the issue at length around their campfires and would keep their distance.

****

Lieutenant Watkin Tench sat on a tree stump on the edge of the forest. The day was particularly fine; the sky was so blue it seemed he could reach up, press his finger into it and leave a mark. He could feel the sun piercing his back and thought about the huge canopy that only weeks before had sheltered the area.

He wasn't staying permanently in the colony; his time in Sydney Cove was for its first years only. So for him, the expedition was a grand adventure. He gazed around, thinking about the progress that had been carved out of the wilderness beside him, and what was still to be done.

What lay to the westward, out there in the wilderness?
Watkin Tench was itching to know...

From where he now sat, he had a view of native canoes out on the water. When they paddled around the bay, they usually had a small fire burning on a pad of hardened clay in their canoe to cook fish as they caught it. They were patient people. The women sat hour after hour, fishing in their canoes, often with a child on their lap.

His mind went back to the early weeks of February, when he and other officers were exploring the harbour. They'd met groups of friendly natives, who laughed, danced and sang with them. The natives had been intrigued by the white men's clothing, believing them to be different layers of skin. There had been curiosity on both sides in the early days and he wondered what had changed.

Through his daydreaming, Tench became aware of the pleasant sounds of native women laughing and singing together as they paddled past.

'It must have been so pleasant here before we arrived,' he thought.

The sun reflecting on the bay, cast shimmery patches of light across the silvery green of the opposite shore. There were so many little inlets still to explore in the harbour.

What was there yet to be discovered?

He peered over his shoulder, squinting against the intensity of light thrown in shafts between the nearby trees. It seemed so vast out there in the forests too. He jotted in his notebook:

'As far as the eye can see to the west, the country is a continuous woodland.'

Yet here they were, huddled into a tiny camp space on the edge of the wilderness, in a mysterious land at the end of the known world.

****

His attention was brought back to reality by a sharp, angry bellow from a convict guard supervising a group of disinterested men digging the ground.

'Keep going you good-for-nothing, lazy, scoundrels! Dig!'

It was true that since landing, some convicts had shown themselves to be dishonest, unreliable rogues. They had to be watched...and pushed, forced and beaten...to get any work out of them.

On the other hand, a percentage of them were decent men and women like Henry and Susannah Kable. The Governor, learning who had what skills and abilities, had assigned convicts jobs suited to their experience. His intention was also to reward those who deserved it.

There was the builder, James Bloodworth with a seven-year sentence for stealing, who had already made an impression on Governor Phillip. He'd shown himself to be a cut above the lazy ones who scratched at the surface of the ground with as little effort as possible. Many of them didn't know a shovel from an axe and didn't want to learn. The Governor suspected that some had deliberately broken or 'lost' their tools. They grumbled and blamed the new land for their problems.

'The ground's too hard. The timber's too tough. There's no clay to make bricks. There's no decent food. Everything's different here!'

But James Bloodworth had initiative. He showed convicts and marines how to build simple huts with material found nearby. Even men who had some idea of building knew there was a lot to learn from Bloodworth. Youngsters like John Hudson, who had lived in London, knew nothing about making or growing anything. It was a new experience for him.

He watched as Bloodworth demonstrated how to make a basic frame with timber from local trees, using poles from the cabbage tree palms that grew around the harbour.

'Now you 'ave to bury the poles deep, and pack earth around the base. See like this.' Bloodworth stamped and rammed the ground till it was packed hard around the upright posts.

'Make sure they don't wobble if ye want ye hut to stay standin' and watch how I fix the roof frame.'

Then he went on to explain what to use for making the walls.

'Now, ye need soft, springy stems or branches to twist in and out, between the posts, like so.' He showed them how to bend and weave the stems sideways through the upright poles to form a wall.

'Then you plaster it over with a thick mud mixture. When it 'ardens it'll keep the wind and rain out...if it's done right,' he added.

John Hudson watched as the roof frame was covered with layers of reeds and rushes that he'd helped gather from around the harbour.

'Lay 'em thick across the roof beams so the rain runs straight off. That's right,' he encouraged the workers under his supervision.

'What about doors and windows?' someone wanted to know.

'Well, till we 'av enough cut timber for doors, and till glass arrives from England, we'll 'ave to make lattice ones. Same as the walls, only in a frame.'

Finally the first little cabbage tree hut was finished.

'It won't last forever, but it'll do till we find better material,' Bloodworth advised.

Soon other huts began to spring up. They were rough dwellings, and some of them leaked in heavy rain, but they would do for now. They were better than tents.

Even the Governor consulted Bloodworth about supervising the building of his own house when suitable material was found. Government House would be made from bricks and stone and have two levels. Plans were already underway.

Another convict proving useful to the Governor was a fisherman, William Bryant. He'd been convicted for smuggling[7] off the coast of England and sentenced to seven years transportation. However he had shown himself to be reliable during the voyage so Phillip had given him an important role as the colony's chief fisherman.

A short time after landing in Sydney Cove, William married Mary, a young woman from the same fishing district in England. She was transported for stealing but also behaved well during the journey from England. Governor Phillip, keen to reward good behaviour, gave permission for the couple to live in a small hut near the water. With William's fishing experience and his ability to supply the colony with extra food, the Governor put him in charge of all fishing boats. As well as overseeing the fishing, he was responsible for repairing and keeping the boats in good condition.

****

Life was promising for William and Mary Bryant at Sydney Cove, but all they thought and spoke about was getting back to England. They still had years of their sentences to serve before they were free to return to their homeland, but that didn't stop them discussing it... and making secret plans.

[7] smuggling = bringing stolen or illegal goods into a country

Chapter 15

Sydney Cove, April 1788

Elizabeth Hayward watched as the Reverend Johnson's hut, being built with cabbage tree poles, began to take shape. As soon as it was finished, it would be her home too. She would move in with the preacher and his wife Mary, as their servant. The hut would have two rooms and she'd sleep in the main room that would also be the kitchen. Already the Reverend called it their 'little cabbage tree cottage'.

'Can you imagine our friends in England staring in amazement at our strange little house,' he said to his wife as they inspected it one day with Elizabeth. 'If only they could see it,' he chuckled.

'Oh, all the blessings we receive,' he added directing the comment to Elizabeth. She wanted to say something cheeky but she reminded herself of Dot's advice to 'mind her manners', and instead replied, 'Yes, Reverend Johnson.'

Part of Elizabeth's work routine was to collect oyster shells from the rocks near the settlement with other convict women. She learnt that the shells would be burnt and crushed into a powder to make lime for mortar.

'What's mortar?' she asked one of the other women.

'It's a thick mixture of water and lime that cements bricks together. Keeps the walls from fallin' down,' she was told. 'It's needed for the Gov'nor's house. It's going to be built of brick 'n stone'.

'Fancy that,' Elizabeth replied. 'The shells we're collectin' now will go into holdin' up the Governor's house.'

****

As the weather cooled, James Bloodworth, the convict builder became even busier. The marines needed to get out of tents and under cover, so the building of their military barracks got under way. Also with winter approaching, weather-proof buildings for storehouses and a hospital were vital, so the building work sped up under his direction. At the same time, he was involved in the groundwork for the Governor's house.

Bricks were already being made a little way from Sydney Cove in an area where good clay had been discovered. The brick-makers had to soften and press the clay with their feet. Then they packed it into brick-molds brought from England, before baking the bricks in kilns to make them rock-hard.

Most of the men working at the brickfield had no experience of the job. They had to be trained and it was backbreaking work. There were no spare horses to pull the carts piled high with bricks, so groups of eight, ten or twelve convicts had to drag the loaded carts. It took hours of hauling along the rough, bumpy tracks to get the bricks to the main site where they were used in the building work. In hot weather, the cart-wheels stirred the dust, choking and blinding the men. When it rained, mud dragged at the wheels and sometimes they got bogged. Then it took hours to get going again.

Other convicts learnt how to cut stone blocks from the hillsides and carve them into the right shape and size for building. Some worked in the sawpits, cutting and preparing the local timber for frames. It didn't take long before material was ready to begin the Governor's six-room house.

****

Esther Abrahams looked around Lieutenant George Johnston's newly completed hut with its bare earth floor, thatched roof and rickety furniture. It was temporary housing until a more suitable place was built, but it was the oddest little place she had ever been inside. She was to be the lieutenant's housekeeper and she would make it as comfortable as possible. He had promised he would look after her and her young daughter Rosanna so she was feeling more confident about their future. Lieutenant Johnston was the Governor's aide de camp, which he explained, meant he was one of his most trusted officers, the Governor's 'right-hand man'.

George Johnston's little hut overlooked the bay and was not far from the site of the Governor's house. Immediately behind, the area was cleared of trees, but then there was thick woodland.

'I still worry about what wild animals may be in that forest, George,' she said when they were alone. 'There's still so much we don't know about this place.'

'Well it so happens, the Governor is planning a trip west, in the direction of the mountains to see what's there. We'll leave this month. He hopes to find an inland river and better areas for farming. As you know the ground's very rocky here,' he added.

Knowing she wasn't wondering about rivers when she spoke of the unknown, George reassured her. 'And as you know, we've not come across any fierce beasts on any exploring trips so far.'

Esther wanted to express concern about him going into wild country, but she knew better. George Johnston was a brave and adventurous officer and she was not his wife, not yet. She was a convict, belonging to the lowest class of people. In England, she was 'scum of the earth'. She knew it was wise to remember her place.

****

In late April, the Governor set off westward with a group of soldiers and officers, including George Johnston. It would be their most promising and challenging trip yet. They were heading into the unknown interior, toward the hazy peaks, already being called the 'blue' mountains. The range of mountains stretched as far as the eye could see to the north and south. It seemed likely a river would lead them through to the mysterious region on the other side.

They headed west first by boat, along the narrowing harbour to reach its source, then on foot across country. They only took supplies for six days, because they had to carry everything they needed. Their tents, weapons, clothes, food and cooking pots were bundled on their backs. They also had to carry water, not knowing if they would come across a river. They also took spare shoes, because on other hikes the rough, rocky country had ruined the men's footwear. One of the officers wrote how he felt in the wilderness the first night.

> *Here in the most wild and distant place that anyone could imagine we washed our shirts and stockings and set up our tents for the night.*

They carried on for four more days but found that the mountains were much further than they first appeared. Their food supply would run out if they continued, so they turned back.

Some things had puzzled them during the trip. They didn't see any natives in the forests though they saw evidence that they'd been there recently. Besides that, the British men wondered what the natives lived on away from the coast. The white men hadn't found a thing to eat while away from Sydney.

They had however found areas of good soil for farming. The place at the head of the harbour looked to be an excellent place for a second mainland settlement. The Governor later named it 'Rose Hill'.

****

Out in the wilderness it had been easy for the native families to avoid the explorers. They had watched the white men trudging through the undergrowth, heard them cursing at the prickly bushes, and huffing and puffing up the rocky slopes and wondered about the heavy loads on their backs.

They noticed their thick body-hugging red jackets restricting their movement and the heavy coverings on their feet and they couldn't understand why men would load themselves up in such a way.

In the forests, it was not difficult for the black people to keep a comfortable distance between themselves and the white men.

****

On the coast, around Sydney Cove, it was a different story. It was becoming more difficult for the black families to cope near the strangers' expanding campsite. They had to go further to gather food and find material needed to make their tools and fishing equipment. As the weather cooled, it became harder to catch enough fish. There was more competition for food.

It wasn't long before they realised they couldn't leave their spears and tools around, as they had before the white people arrived. Their equipment was essential for fishing and hunting, and they were constantly going missing. Their patience was being tested.

****

Reports continued to come to the Governor about convicts injuring natives and stealing their belongings. So, at the end of April, when two convicts were attacked, and one speared very badly, the Governor suspected they had brought the harm on themselves. It was payback for what they had done.

The Governor wanted to let the natives know that he didn't approve of the theft of their things. He wanted to explain to them that the men who stole from them were 'convicts', and already a disgraced class of people. He wanted to show them that the white people who harmed them would be punished.

But what was to be done about it?
How could he communicate his concern and his intentions to them?

Chapter 16

Sydney Cove, May 1788

Susannah Kable felt the cold morning air on her face as she stepped outside to begin her day. She would work with other women making wooden pegs to fix shingles[8] to the hospital roof. Doctor White wanted it completely covered before the winter set in.

She shivered, wondering how much colder Sydney Cove would get.

'It's the first of May,' she called inside to Henry. 'It's springtime back home.'

'Ay lass, it is,' Henry replied, knowing the memory would prompt a wave of homesickness, of her longing to be back in England.

'There'll be carpets of golden daffodils everywhere, and bluebells all through the forest and along the roadsides,' she stared into the distance recalling her childhood. She saw herself collecting armfuls of wildflowers to decorate the house and later dancing in the village with the other girls. 'I loved springtime back home.'

'Ay lass, and if you were in England now, do ye think you'd be free to enjoy May Day? I don't think so.' He had come to stand next to her, overlooking the shimmering bay.

'You're right, Henry. Best get on with it,' she said with a weak smile.

Susannah, with her toddler balanced on her hip, walked down the slope to cross the little stream dividing the settlement. She put him down as they reached the water.

---

[8] Shingles are small, thin, pieces of wood cut to lay over a frame to cover a roof.

'Now hold my hand tight as we cross the water,' she urged.

'Mama where fishies?' he squatted by the edge but she gently tugged him to his feet. 'Not now Harry, Mama has work to do.'

As they made their way over the narrowest section of water by means of log planks, she reminded herself they were better off in Sydney Cove. Little Harry could play in the sunshine; he would grow up free. But she still missed her homeland.

****

In the first week of May, Henry told his wife about a milestone for the colony. The first stone of the Governor's house would be set in place with a brass panel attached to mark the date, 15th May 1788.

The same week the cornerstone was laid for the Governor's house, Henry arrived home to receive his own good news.

'We're going to have another baby, Henry,' Susannah announced. 'A little girl would be wonderful. We could call her Dianna after ye mum,' she added.

'Ah, lass,' Henry nodded. He thought about his mother so far away in England. She would like that, he thought.

****

Governor Phillip was pleased with the progress of the building work, especially with the start on his own house. However at the end of May an officer came to see him in an agitated state. Judging by his distress, Phillip guessed he was bringing bad news.

'What is it man?' the Governor asked abruptly.

'Sir, I went up harbour to collect rushes from two convicts I'd left there...' the man was breathless. 'I'd left them at the spot with a tent to cut the reeds for thatching my house. When I got there I found the tent but not the m-men.' He paused to steady his voice. 'Seeing a trail of blood near the tent, I followed it to the mangrove bushes where I found both men dead. They'd been speared, Sir. It was a terrible sight, Sir.'

It was disturbing news, but the Governor's first thought was that the men had brought the attack on themselves. Dealings with natives had shown no signs of trouble. Just after news of the attack, a party of native men had paddled alongside *HMS Sirius* in a friendly manner and agreed to the novelty of being shaved by the sailors. Afterward they landed on the western point of the cove, near Lieutenant Dawes' observatory, and examined everything there with great attention. Then they went away peaceably.

'It seems unlikely they would do that if they were worried about us taking revenge for the murders,' the Governor said to George Johnston. 'I think a thorough investigation is needed.'

'Yes Sir. Some of the rush-cutters' clothes and all their tools were taken so if we can trace them, we could identify the guilty party.'

Had natives done this?
If so, what was the reason behind the attack?

The killings couldn't be ignored and the Governor believed, by catching the culprits with the tools, it might be possible to discover why it had happened. He began preparation for a party of well-armed officers, including himself and George Johnston, to leave the following day.

News of the murdered convicts filtered around the settlement, causing anxiety for those who had to venture into bushland away from the main camp. Esther looked over her shoulder when she went to collect water, and stayed in a group when collecting the vine they used to make sweet tea. But when George told her he was going on an expedition to find the killers, she kept her fears to herself.

'We still don't know the intentions of the natives toward us,' George told Esther. 'They continue to avoid our settlement, except for short visits to satisfy their curiosity.'

'But why do they attack us?' Esther asked, trying to hide her fear.

'So far it seems they only attack our people after one of their own has been injured by some of our thieving convicts. But the killings can't be ignored.' He repeated the Governor's words. 'We must find out why this is happening.'

Fourteen-year-old John Hudson heard about the deaths and went about his business. He was used to convicts boasting about their thefts of native tools, which they called 'finds'. They talked openly in front of him because he was 'just a lad'. He knew the convicts sold them to the sailors returning to England, and because three of the ships had left earlier in May, he wasn't surprised that some of the fools had gone too far.

John didn't dwell on the incident because he had other things on his mind. He was involved in preparing a huge bonfire the Governor had said they could build for June 4th. As he dragged and stacked branches on top of logs, he watched with satisfaction as the pile grew. His earlier life, climbing inside grimy London chimneys, was fading to a distant memory.

Chapter 17

Sydney Cove, June 1788

At daybreak on the first day of June, the Governor set out with a small party of twelve armed men for the place where the murders had happened. Finding no further clues, and not a trace of the natives ever being there, they headed toward Botany Bay. One of the officers wrote about their journey:

> *A little before sun-set, after a long and tiring march, we arrived on the coast of Botany Bay where we saw eleven canoes with fires burning within and two people fishing in each. Here we pitched our tents, and built large fires in front and at the rear of us because the air was so icy.*

The next morning they packed up their tents after a sleepless night. It was bitterly cold and the ground, white with frost, crackled beneath their frozen feet. They saw about fifty canoes pulled up on the beach, but not a native person in sight. Governor Phillip decided there was no point staying any longer, as the natives were apparently not willing to meet.

Finding a well-worn pathway, the men began the march back to Sydney Cove and had walked for only a short time when, all of a sudden, they heard voices. As they rounded a bend in the track, they came upon a great crowd of natives who seemed just as astonished at seeing them.

Everything changed so quickly that the Governor hardly had time to halt his men before a number of armed warriors stood on the track in front of them. One of the officers described what happened next in his journal:

> *Every one of them was armed with a long spear, a shield made of bark, and either a large club, or a stone hatchet.*
>
> *At first they seemed angry, and made signs for us to go back, but when they saw the Governor advance towards them unarmed, and with his hands opened wide they came up to him with confidence, and received some things from him, such as fish-hooks, beads, and a looking-glass. Most of the women and children were kept at a distance, except one or two who came forward for presents.*
>
> *There appeared more than three hundred of them in this bay, all armed, so the governor ordered the soldiers to be prepared. As already mentioned, these people seem to dislike red coats and those who carry weapons, but on this occasion they showed very little fear or distrust. In fact, in a short time, they mixed with us, and led us to a stream of water, where they drank from it to show us that it was good.*
>
> *As we were walking, one of our men picked up a mushroom, but the natives made signs to throw it away as it was not good to eat.*

Before the Englishmen left to continue their trek to Sydney Cove, the Governor exchanged two metal hand-axes for some of their stone axes and two spears.

As they began their march homeward, one of the warriors went ahead of them to the top of a hill, where he stopped and holding his arms above his head, he made a loud call into the valley.

As soon as the Governor and his group reached him, they saw another large body of natives below in the next bay. Their new friend indicated he wanted to take the Englishmen down the hill to introduce them. But Governor Phillip was keen to return to Sydney which lay in the opposite direction, so he declined his offer. By way of thanks, the Governor gave him a bird they had shot earlier. It was all he had left to show appreciation.

On the way back to Sydney Cove, the Englishmen discussed their experience. It was the largest number of native people they'd seen together since their arrival in the country. They were very aware of how dangerous their situation had been.

'We were greatly outnumbered. We didn't stand a chance if they'd wanted to kill us. Only twelve of us and hundreds of them.'

Phillip considered the actions and attitude of the people they'd met.

'I saw nothing to indicate any of them were involved in the attack on the rush-cutters,' he said to his officers, and they all agreed.

They also debated possible reasons why the natives were gathered in such a large group. Some thought they were preparing to go to war with a nearby tribe. Others imagined they'd assembled for a burial, a marriage, or some religious meeting.

****

On his arrival in Sydney, the Governor heard fresh evidence about the rush-cutter incident. It seemed that a few days before the men were speared, they had stolen a canoe belonging to the natives. Also, there were rumours that one of the natives had been murdered and others wounded by white men.

The Governor decided that the deaths were related. The attack on the rush-cutters was a payback killing.

> 'I'm more convinced than ever of the importance of treating them with confidence,' he announced. 'We must learn from this, and overcome the problems between us, whatever they are.'

****

Around Warran (Sydney Cove) as time went by, some of the natives also began to change their attitude about the strangers. Through meetings with white people *outside* their settlement, they found that not all white skinned people were the same. It seemed wrong to judge the whole lot because of the things they saw at the main camp.

They had met friendly white men and women when the strangers walked from their settlement into the nearby forest. And some white people, both men and women, visited their family campsites where the groups sat together around their fires. They danced and sang together for pure fun. They didn't need to know or understand the words to enjoy the atmosphere. The white people had invited them to go back with them into the place they called 'Sydney' but they would not go there. It was a strange place where the redcoats paced with their *gooroobeera (fire stick weapons)*. No, they would not go into that place, but they welcomed the peaceful white people, the ones without weapons.

There was also the white man they'd heard called 'Dawes', living alone near his strange shelter on the western point. He acted differently to the 'red coats' in the main camp. As they paddled past his place on the headland, they saw the quiet man studying the plants growing in the bush around his hut. They saw him watching the stars move across the night sky and they saw him observing them, as they fished from the rocks. It seemed that he wanted to connect with them. They would visit Dawes for an extended stay when the time was right.

****

Meanwhile piles of timber had been growing in Sydney Cove in preparation for bonfires to celebrate King George of England's birthday, on June 4th. The Governor saw it as an opportunity to spread some cheer by announcing the date as a public holiday. All work stopped for the day to allow everyone to enjoy the occasion. He allowed some grog[9] from his own supply, to every convict and soldier to drink to His Majesty's health. The military band paraded and played 'God Save the King' and throughout the day, the ships *Sirius* and *Supply* fired volleys of twenty-one guns from their cannons. The first volley was early in the morning, then again at one o'clock and finally at sunset. The officers ate a hearty meal with the Governor consisting of pork, duck, chicken, fish, kangaroo, salads, pies and preserved fruits. George Worgan, one of the doctors, described the evening celebrations in his journal:

> *About 5 o'clock we walked out to visit the bonfires. The convicts had been two days collecting for one of them which was piled up high round a large tree. It was really a great sight. Here, the convicts were gathered, singing.*

John Hudson stood admiring the bonfire he had helped to build. It felt like he lived in a different world now. If only the boys from his chimneysweep days in London could see him standing before this crackling blaze, beneath an immense star-speckled sky. He looked up to see the Governor, His Excellency, walking toward his bonfire.

[9] grog = a weak alcoholic drink

As other convicts saw the Governor approaching, they gave three loud cheers, and switched from belting out their folk songs to join in singing *'God Save the King'*. The mood was relaxed as the voices raised in unison. The Governor didn't just stand at a distance and watch, he actually came and stood by the bonfire among them.

Fourteen-year-old Elizabeth Hayward was standing within a group of women thoroughly enjoying the familiar songs from home, when she saw the Governor approach. As the crowd began singing the British anthem, she joined in, though she didn't know or understand all the words.

'God save great George our King. Long live our noble king.
God save the King. Send him victorious, happy and glorious,
long to reign over us, God save the King.'

Never had she enjoyed herself so much, despite a lot of the meaning going over her head. Old Dot, sitting on a log nearby, seemed to know the words. In fact, there were tears in her eyes.

'Ah, the old country. Old England calls me,' she mumbled. 'I'm goin' 'ome ye know Lizzie. One day I'm goin' 'ome.' Elizabeth just nodded.

Little Harry Kable was now over two years old and beamed up at his father Henry, absorbing all the excitement around him.

'Big fire dada,' he shouted, his face flushed with heat and pleasure.

'Ay lad. A very big fire,' his father replied, enjoying the scene of convicts singing.

Henry felt thankful for all he had. Susannah was his wife and nothing could change that. She was close beside him and soon they would have their second child. This day had given him hope for his children's future, but one thing still worried and annoyed him. They had not received the parcel of goods donated to them in England. He must follow up on that.

****

For most of the convicts enjoying the King's birthday celebration, the event felt unreal. Their campsite was a speck on the edge of a vast wilderness, as far away from their home as they could imagine. They were in fact at the end of the known world. Yet, here they were, a group of prisoners gathered around a bonfire, singing to their King in a distance land. They were celebrating outdoors under a crisp, clear sky, with their Governor standing in their midst.

****

For the Aboriginal families around Sydney Cove, the noise, the fires and the singing had again been impossible to ignore. They looked on from their viewing places with amazement. They'd heard the white men's guns firing many times before, they'd seen the redcoats parading and the workers herded together but they had never seen or heard so much laughter in the white camp since they'd arrived.

The event was the closest they'd ever seen to their own *caribberie* [10] celebration with its enjoyment of song, dance and music.

Maybe there was some hope for these white people.

****

Eight-year-old Nanberry also heard the loud laughter, music and singing coming from the settlement in the next cove. He listened to the comments of surprise from his elders and wondered if he would ever get to visit the strangers' campsite.

Little did he know that one day he would do much more than that.

[10] caribberie = corroboree (a special dance)

Chapter 18

Sydney Cove, July - August, 1788

During July, four of the hired ships that had brought the convicts to Sydney Cove prepared to sail for England. News of their departure started a flurry of letter writing. Everyone at Sydney Cove desperately wanted to hear from their family and friends in England but no ships had arrived yet with news. At least by writing, they could let their relatives know they were still alive, and tell them about life on the edge of the world.

Some letters described the prospects the new land offered them, while others painted a negative picture of life at Sydney Cove. Major Ross, who was not on good terms with the Governor, believed he spoke for everyone in the colony when he wrote: 'There is not a man in this place that does not wish to return home.'

Others wrote about the peculiar animals living near their settlement. They described a bird, called 'emu', that was taller than a man, could outrun a dog, but couldn't fly.
They wrote of the Governor's pet native pup, which the natives called 'dingo'.

Lieutenant Clark wrote to his wife, Betsy about the strangest animal of all, the kangaroo. He also told her about things the settlers ate:

> *The kangaroo is the most extraordinary animal that I ever saw. It has a pocket at the front of its belly to carry its baby. They are plentiful and many are shot and make very good eating.*
>
> *Nothing goes to waste here – snakes and lizards get eaten but I cannot yet bring myself to stomach them. Crows and parrots and any sort of bird I do try as they are better than the salt beef we are limited to otherwise...*

Some convicts, like John Hudson, didn't have anyone to write to, even if they were able to use a pen. But if he could, John would say he never wanted to return to his life in London. He was fourteen now but his body was still stunted. In Sydney Cove, his undersized frame had freed him from heavy labour so it didn't bother him. His work varied. Sometimes he helped gather reeds used for thatching, and some days he helped on the building sites. If he was lucky, he went on the fishing boats with William Bryant. The sense of freedom he felt out on the harbour was beyond words.

John had suspicions about William Bryant. Something was going on that shouldn't be; secret packages handed over, winks and nods. Nobody ever thought that he noticed stuff – he was just young John.

✦✦✦✦

With the approaching departure of the ships, the issue of the Kable's missing parcel of goods came to a head.

'I've asked to speak to the Gov'nor about it,' he announced one night to Susannah. 'It's not right. Those things were given to us.'

'But Henry, the Governor's not goin' to be bothered with that. He's got more pressing things to worry about.'

'Well, I have to try. Once the ships leave, there's no way we'll get our stuff. And the master of that ship should answer for it.'

Susannah admired her husband's boldness but thought they had no chance. They were convicts, and convicts had no rights. But Henry's nerve paid off. The Governor knew the couple had attracted publicity in England. He was aware of the goods donated to the Kables, and was prepared to listen to Henry's complaint.

At that time, all ships leaving the colony had supposedly been unloaded, but according to Kable, their property had gone missing. Only a few books had been delivered to the couple after Henry had enquired earlier. He now appealed to the Governor.

'Your Excellency, I'm wondering if anything can be done about it?' Henry asked in his politest tone.

'Leave it with me. I'll make some enquiries,' the Governor replied.

Governor Phillip, after asking some questions, decided to order a court hearing. The accusation was that the master of *Alexander* had not delivered the property as he'd been hired to do. John White formed part of the court, and wrote what happened:

A civil court was arranged to hear a complaint against the master of the Alexander transport, by Henry Kable and Susannah his wife, the Norwich convicts who excited so much public attention in England. The complaint was for the non-delivery of a parcel sent aboard containing clothes, books and other things, to the value of twenty pounds.

The court, after deducting five pounds (the value of the books received), gave a verdict in favour of the couple and judged the master of the transport to fully compensate the loss of the convicts, amounting to fifteen pounds.

This was the first civil court case ever held in the colony and it caused a stir in Sydney Cove. Convicts had no rights at all in Britain, but the court had decided that on the other side of the world, they would do things differently.

'Well I never thought it possible,' said Susannah when she heard the outcome.

And that was the comment heard all around the settlement.

****

For Henry and Susannah, the future was encouraging. Neither of them could write so Henry asked someone to write a letter for him to his mother in England, to let her know of his good fortune:

> *I am, thank God, very easily situated. The officers have been so pleased with my conduct that they continue me in the office of an overseer over the women convicts. Our little boy Harry is a promising little fellow and learning every day.*
>
> *We have a good and healthy climate but very heavy rains and strong claps of thunder. Our summer is very hot and our winter begins in May. It is day here, when it is night for you. We have a little garden, which supplies us with plenty of cabbage and turnips.*

The Kables were in a good position, but they knew uncertainty still lay ahead for them and for the settlement. They were growing a few vegetables next to their hut, but the soil was not dark and rich like England's and the seasons were confusing.

'I 'ave to keep telling me self it's NOT summer here in July. It's the middle of winter,' Susannah said as she sat mending their clothes.

'Ah, but the climate's hard to beat,' added Henry smiling. 'We 'ave to keep lookin' on the bright side, lass. Count our blessin's as the Reverend says.'

Susannah knew there was still a lot of adjusting to do if they were to make a successful life for themselves in such different surroundings. She also realised she'd made progress. When they'd first landed, spiders and beetles made her scream, but lately she just brushed them away. Now she was used to the possums living in the trees near their hut, but in the early days she'd trembled in fear seeing one descend nearby to begin its evening activities. At first, she lay awake terrified by the night sounds. Now she knew these furry bush animals were harmless. Each evening, she looked up to greet mother and baby possum with a warning smile.

'Hello, possums. Stay away from our vegie garden now. Go, shoo.'

****

Henry had a vision for their future and talked about ways of bettering themselves. He was always planning.

'Down the track the colony will need ships and traders. And...'

'Well let's just go slowly Henry,' Susannah said, stroking little Harry to sleep. 'Right now we need to focus on growing food.'

The Kables rose early every day to work in their garden and improve their home before they began their assigned jobs. If they had the energy, they did the same in the evenings. They were not only working for themselves, but for little Harry and their second child, already well on the way. They knew, above everything else, they must stay on the right side of the law.

****

In August rain arrived. It came down so hard it was difficult to get around the settlement. All the tracks became muddy bogs. At the brickfield, the firing kilns caved in and many of the bricks were destroyed. The constant downpour made working impossible, so throughout the settlement, work was officially suspended. Convicts huddled in their shelters in damp clothes, watching with dismal expressions, as trickles of water turned to cascades pouring through their thatched roofs.

The Reverend Johnson's hut leaked so badly that water ran through like a little stream. It was cold and miserable and Elizabeth Hayward decided she didn't like living there.

'Come on. Come on, girl. Get something to soak that up,' the Reverend ordered as he splashed about ankle deep in muddy water.

Elizabeth understood he was flustered but he didn't have to take it out on her and she wanted to say so. She felt she would never be good enough for the Reverend, but she did like his wife, the Ma'am. She never complained. Mrs Johnson was kind and spoke with a soft voice, and to Elizabeth's delight, she was expecting a baby.

The Reverend on the other hand, was always telling her to 'count her blessings'. When she didn't water the vegetables enough or pull the weeds to his satisfaction, he scolded her. He set high standards.

'The Lord says those who don't work, don't eat, remember Lizzie.'

'Just coz 'e likes diggin' an' plantin' in the garden, it don't mean everyone else 'as to,' she complained later to Old Dot.

'Just mind ye tongue, or you'll earn y'self a lashing, girl,' Dot told her, knowing she'd been close to getting one a few times.

The Johnson's cabbage tree hut had two small rooms with a thin partition between the quarters. The Reverend and his wife slept in the side room and Elizabeth slept in the kitchen. Each night she laid her sack mattress, filled with leaves and ferns, in front of the fire. Before she drifted off to sleep, she sometimes heard the vicar complaining about the convicts' attitude.

'They're so blind, so hardened and so foolish. I'm sorry to see so little good done amongst the poor souls,' he said in a hushed voice.

Mary Johnson listened silently, then Elizabeth would hear her reassuring him with her calm voice that he was doing all he could.

'Mm,' Elizabeth thought. 'Maybe 'e should try a convict's life.'

****

Whenever Elizabeth said anything against the Reverend, Susannah Kable would defend him. She pointed out how he supported the idea of Isabella Rawson teaching the convicts' children.

'He does 'is best for the little ones. He 'asn't got an easy job ye' know. Isabella told me the Reverend praised the way she's showin' the little ones their letters. She looks after our Harry an' teaches 'im while we work. He already knows some letters 'an he's not yet three. He's a bright little one,' she added proudly.

Elizabeth knew Susannah was right about the Reverend doing his best for the children. He'd brought books from England and he'd encouraged her to learn her letters. Maybe one day she'd succeed. Isabella had offered to teach her too but she was busy with her little band of students. Isabella was also expecting a baby herself.

****

Isabella Rawson was in her element with children around her. When her baby had died on the voyage aboard *Lady Penrhyn*, she'd thought she would never feel happy again. But seeing her little students make letters with their fingers in the sand, she felt joyful.

She was still serving her sentence, but the Reverend had encouraged her to put her teaching skills to use. He said he would supply little books when the children were able to read.

Isabella was feeling weary now that her baby's birth was getting near. She was looking forward to motherhood but she knew there were hard times ahead. Her baby's father, a marine, would not marry her. He'd go back to England when he could, and she'd be left to bring up a child alone. At least she'd have a baby of her own to love, at last.

****

As winter turned to spring, the settlers began to enjoy mild days. Brilliant spring flowers appeared throughout the bushland and the convicts picked armfuls to decorate their little huts. There were huge showy red blossoms the native people called 'waratah' and small trees covered in flowers that looked like bottlebrushes of many shades. Bright yellow fluffy balls lit up the hillsides and filled the air with a sweet fragrance. The sky was a rich endless blue.

The lightness of springtime spurred on James Ruse's feeling of optimism. He sensed an opportunity for a hardworking convict farmer like him was just around the corner.

Chapter 19

Rose Hill (Burramatta) September - November, 1788

After the departure of the hired First Fleet ships for England, the Governor turned his attention to food production. The wheat seed planted at Sydney Cove had not done well, and he believed the ground too rocky to grow enough food for the colony. He decided to send Captain John Hunter in *HMS Sirius* to Africa to buy extra supplies. He knew it could take six months for him to return with provisions, so meanwhile they must try to become self-sufficient. If they didn't grow more food there'd be a serious shortage. Further inland to the west where the harbour narrowed, the soil was better, so he began planning a settlement at the place he called Rose Hill.

He sent a hundred convicts, guarded by a captain and twenty marines to begin constructing huts, a storehouse for provisions, and a small fort for the soldiers. There would also be a wharf built for delivering supplies. The white men wasted no time in clearing and preparing the ground for corn and wheat.

****

At the head of the harbour the Burramatta people were troubled by the arrival of so many new people. The strangers began clearing away trees, which meant the material for native tools and for making canoes was removed. The riverbanks they visited to dig for tasty yams were trampled, and the fern used for medicine was ripped out to make way for the white men's crops. Their hunting grounds were wiped out as animals' habitats were destroyed.

The white leader had not consulted with them. The new arrivals had taken the land next to the river for themselves, so it became more and more difficult for the natives to catch eels and other fish along the riverbanks. It was now obvious the strangers were not going to share resources. They had come to take over.

This kind of dilemma was completely new to the people at the head of the harbour. Their ancestors had lived undisturbed on the riverbank for thousands of years and had never faced a situation of this kind. They'd never needed a large body of fighting men like the red coats to guard their territory. They'd never before had to defend their land in this way.

They traded with native groups from other areas, respecting their boundaries. It was true, they had conflict and battles with neighbouring warriors, but there was tribal law. They knew what to expect. Food gathering methods varied from place to place, but they shared the same understanding of their country, and the importance of taking only what was needed. The young men discussed all these issues as they fished further along the river.

The ways of the white people were hard to understand. To tear up the land with no thought for what they were destroying was crazy.

If they cut down trees, how would they supply their future needs?

They would wait for an opportunity to let the white leader know they were not happy. But for now, with the sudden disruption to their way of life, their concern was finding enough food to survive.

****

As soon as James Ruse heard about arrangements for the farming settlement at Rose Hill, he knew it was time to put forward his plan. He believed it was possible and just hoped the Governor would give him a chance. He applied to speak with him about his idea.

'I grew up in the business of farming, Your Excellency,' he began, nervously clutching his hat with both hands. Phillip nodded.

He knew Ruse was from a rural background and was hard working.

Seeing he had the Governor's attention, Ruse launched into the plan he'd rehearsed so often in his head. He went on to suggest that, with a plot of ground, help to clear the land and a supply of seed and animal stock, he believed he could support himself within a set time. He knew it was a bold scheme for a convict to put to a Governor but he remembered the Governor's first speech and his promise of 'encouragement for good conduct'.

Phillip looked the man over. He could see he had initiative and had shown he could be trusted. He needed men with drive, and by rewarding this man, it may encourage others to be more motivated.

'I will give your plan some serious thought Ruse. You may go now.'

The scheme appealed to Governor Phillip for several reasons. The more he thought about it, the experiment excited him.

****

Phillip outlined his plan to his officers, knowing some would disagree.

'As you all know, negative views exist about this country.' He looked round knowing some officers in the room had that exact opinion.

'Some say we will never succeed here,' he paused to make a point. 'Some believe the ground will never produce enough food to keep us going. Such bad opinions seem to be spreading and are having a harmful effect on our people,' he waited again before continuing.

'But the man Ruse is convinced that he can prove otherwise. He believes he can become self-sufficient if he gets help at the start. He's convinced me that he will overcome whatever obstacles he has to face. I am going to agree to this experiment and I would like you all to show support for the idea.'

The Governor arranged for Ruse to move to Rose Hill and begin the challenge. Later the Governor's secretary wrote down the details:

> *His Excellency, had two acres of ground cleared of timber, and a small hut built for him. He provided the tools needed for cultivating his ground, some grain to sow it and a small quantity of livestock to begin with.*
>
> *The man himself promised to be industrious and to overcome whatever difficulties might lie in his way. Rewarding him, was holding out encouragement to other good characters.*

The area of land cleared for James Ruse became known as 'Experiment Farm'. The success of the project was as important to the Governor as it was to Ruse. Besides holding him up as an example of a deserving character, he was keen to see how long it would take for an active man, with some government assistance, to support himself on his land.

James Ruse was about to have an opportunity that would never be possible in England, in his lifetime.

****

Around the time James Ruse was beginning a new phase of his life at Rose Hill, Mary Johnson was giving birth to her firstborn child. The Reverend was very anxious and fussed around, telling Elizabeth to do this and do that. But nothing could change the result. When Mary gave birth to her little son, he was already dead.

'Oh, poor, poor Mrs. Johnson! I never felt more sorry for anyone in me life,' Elizabeth told old Dot and Susannah. 'I even felt for the Reverend. He was so sad, but I didn't know what to say or do.'

'There's not much you can say at a time like that,' Susannah said, patting her belly. Her own baby was due very soon.

At the beginning of December 1788, Susannah and Henry Kable had a beautiful little girl added to the family. They called her Dianna after Henry's mother. Susannah felt so lucky to have two healthy children.

****

Meanwhile at Rose Hill, the new British settlement led to the movement of the Burramatta people away to other places. Native families soon began living at a place known as 'the flats' between the head of the river and Sydney harbour. Others went to live along the creeks to the north of their territory.

At the time, the Governor seemed unaware of the impact Rose Hill was having on the native families. He'd hoped some would visit and be attracted to live in the new settlement after the white men began their building work. He firmly believed in his plan of showing them the advantages of civilization. He wanted to demonstrate that invasions into their territory would be worth it when they saw the benefits the British could offer them. He went back to considering the daring plan he had thought of months earlier.

Natives must be brought into the settlements and stay long enough to see how good life could be for them living with the white settlers.

By the end of the year, he had convinced himself that his plan made sense. He discussed his intention of kidnapping some natives with Lieutenant George Johnston.

'It is the last resort. It would be much better if they would come willingly into the settlement, but if it's done in a way that doesn't cause alarm, it will turn out to be the kindest trick we could use.'

'How and when do you plan this to happen, Sir?'

'The details of how and when I shall leave to you Lieutenant. Just make sure it's done in a way that does not create alarm among them.'

On the last day of 1788, Lieutenant Johnston, with a small party of armed men, left Sydney Cove by boat to carry out the Governor's instructions to seize and carry off some of the natives.

Chapter 20

Sydney Cove, December 31st 1788

Lieutenant Johnston and his men headed across the harbour where they saw a group of men gathered on the beach. The natives waded out to meet them, unaware of the trickery about to happen.

Attracted by the friendly behaviour of the white men who held up gifts, they came quite close to the boats. Then the white men rushed at them and seized two men, who were wrestled toward the boat. One of the victims however, by dragging his attacker into deeper water managed to struggle from his grip. The other man was pulled into the boat, kicking and screaming. His friends were at first shocked by what happened and took off back to the beach. But seeing someone was being taken captive, they began throwing spears, stones and whatever they had at the boat.

****

Surrounded by white strangers, the captive in the boat was in pure panic. When he realised he was separated from his friends and relatives, he began the most piercing cries of distress.

On the journey back across the harbour he wondered what the white men planned to do with him. He'd heard stories about the things that happened in their campsite, but when they offered him fish, he felt relieved. They weren't going to murder him - not yet anyway.

When the boat arrived at Sydney Cove, he saw the white men's settlement up close for the first time. He had entered another world.

When they led him from the boat, his legs felt weak with fear. He was now in the territory of strangers, and had no idea what to expect, or what they planned for him.

A white man came forward, and with words and gestures told him he had nothing to fear. Still bound with ropes he was led through a crowd of people, all clearly excited to see him. With the strangers surrounding him, it was difficult to breathe.

'Step back. Give the poor man some space,' someone yelled.

He didn't understand the words but was grateful when people moved back allowing a clear pathway. As they walked on, the white men pointed at things and said words.

As they came to the white leader's house, he jumped with fright at a sudden sound above his head as they entered.

'Bell,' someone said. 'It's just a bell.' He laughed nervously when a white man pointed to the object.

Once inside, images of people, animals and birds were shown to him and he was told a new word each time. He nodded and remembered the words.

Why had the white people brought him to this place?

****

Next he was led to the Governor's new two-storey brick house, which was still under construction. As he approached the building he saw people leaning from a window on the upper level and gave a shout of astonishment at the possibility of people being up there.

Later, when officers began gathering in the Governor's dining room, the native man became very anxious. Something about the situation deeply disturbed him, but the white men didn't learn what it was until they'd eaten their meal. One of the men at the table later told other officers the reason for the native man's great distress.

'The poor man was so frightened that he wouldn't eat anything. After dinner he was much more relaxed, and we learnt afterward that he'd thought we were going to eat HIM.'

'The natives think WE are cannibals?' someone asked.

'It seems so.' The thought of such a thing caused general laughter.

After the ordeal of believing he was about to be eaten, the man's fear lessened, but there were more trials to come. Lieutenant Watkin Tench wrote about what happened to him next:

In the afternoon his hair was closely cut and combed, and his beard shaved; but he would not allow this to happen until he had seen it done to another person. Then he was put into a tub of water where he was washed from head to foot with soap. After a shirt, a jacket and a pair of trousers were put on him.

He appeared to be about thirty years old. His voice was gentle, though broken and interrupted by fear and panic. When his natural tone could be heard, he pronounced the names of things we taught him very well.

At first the native man withheld his name, but later the white men learnt it was Arabanoo. That night he was locked in a small building close to the guardhouse, with a reliable convict to keep check on him. It had been one of the most frightening days he had ever experienced.

The following morning Arabanoo was very dejected, and in an effort to lift his spirits he was shown around the settlement and taken to Lieutenant Dawes' observatory on the western peninsula. But from there he saw the smoke from the campfires of his people on the far shore. With a deep sigh of sadness, he spoke a single phrase:

'Gweeun.' (the fires of my people)

As it was New Year's Day, all the officers were invited to the Governor's table. Watkin Tench was there, and noted that although Arabanoo was still unhappy, he had a good appetite and ate a fair share of fish and roast pork. He wrote about him later in his journal:

> *Bread and salt meat he smelled at, but would not taste.*
> *Our wine and liquor he treated in the same manner and*
> *would drink nothing but water. On being shown that he*
> *should not wipe his hands on the chair that he sat on,*
> *he used a towel given to him with great cleanliness and*
> *good manners.*

To everyone's surprise, when the meal ended with a song by one of the officers, Arabanoo stretched out on the floor, put his hat under his head, and fell asleep. To the Governor, it seemed the man was adjusting well to his new situation.

Maybe his daring kidnap plan was going to work after all.

Chapter 21

Sydney Cove, January - May 1789

Early in the new year the Governor took Arabanoo down the harbour by boat hoping to show his people that he wasn't hurt and to see if they would come and talk with him. When the boat approached one of the coves, the natives quickly retreated. But on seeing Arabanoo, they returned to the shore. When Arabanoo caught sight of his friends, his eyes filled with tears. Watkin Tench wrote the details:

> *Our ignorance of their language prevented us from knowing all that they said, but it was easy to see that his friends asked him why he did not jump overboard and rejoin them.*
>
> *He only sighed and pointed to the fetter on his leg by which he was bound.*

****

During the first weeks of Arabanoo's time in Sydney Cove, James Ruse was busy clearing his land at Rose Hill, so young John Hudson gave him all the details of the native's arrival.

'He's about your age, I s'pose. Not tall, but strong lookin'. At first he looked terrified when everyone crowded around 'im, not that I blame 'im. But he seems alright now.'

Over the following weeks, Arabanoo began to settle down and quickly gained popularity with everyone at Sydney Cove, especially the children.

When little Harry Kable stood a short distance away watching him eat something, Arabanoo signaled for him to come closer. He drew the little boy toward him gently and offered him his food, talking to him with a soft, kind voice.

'You should see 'im,' Susannah told her husband. 'He's so warm 'n caring with all the little ones. They follow 'im 'n flock round 'im.'

****

Through January, Arabanoo took trips around the harbour with the Governor and pointed to different headlands and creeks willingly giving their names. That was when the British learnt that his people's name for Sydney Cove was 'Warran'.

He freely told the Governor about the customs of his people and seemed resigned that the white leader was keeping him in Sydney Cove to show him things he thought useful for his people.

By February, he was noticeably more comfortable with his situation. A favourite pastime for him and the officers during the evenings was language lessons. They would sit around the Governor's table taking turns at pointing and saying the names of things in each language.

'Mee diee,' (What's this?) Arabanoo asked, pointing to water.
'Bado,' (water) the Governor replied, and Arabanoo nodded.
'Budycree,' (Good) he told the Governor, and they all cheered.

During the conversations, Lieutenant Dawes listened and wrote the words in each language. He had plans to write a language notebook.

Bado	= *water*	*Budyeree*	= *good*
Gweeun	= *fire*	*Mee diee*	= *What's this?*

Arabanoo had a sense of humour and appeared happy to be the subject of a joke, but he wouldn't allow the British men to treat him as if they were better or superior to him. He expected them to show respect. Watkin Tench gave his opinion on Arabanoo's outlook.

> *Although of a gentle and easy-going temper, we soon discovered that he would not allow disrespect.*
>
> *He knew he was under our power, but he held strongly to his pride and belief in himself. If the slightest insult were made to him, he would return it with interest.*

The men were gradually beginning to understand each other's ways. Governor Phillip believed his experiment with Arabanoo was going well. But so far, not one of his countrymen had shown any sign of following him into the settlement. What occurred next did not help.

****

A group of sixteen convicts left their work at the brickfield without permission, with the idea of stealing native spears and fishing gear. Armed with their work tools, they marched toward Botany Bay. When the convicts reached the bay, a large body of natives was waiting for them. They'd seen trouble coming. As a result of the clash, one white man was killed and seven seriously wounded. The Governor was furious and questioned the convicts about the cause of the conflict. At first, all the convicts stuck to the same story:

'We were minding our business, quietly picking leaves to make tea when, without warning, we were attacked by natives!'

Finally, after more questioning, someone admitted the truth and the whole bunch were flogged. Governor Phillip wanted Arabanoo to know that he would not allow or ignore the theft of native equipment, or attacks on them. He wanted him to witness the punishment of the culprits. But as Arabanoo watched the beatings, he showed signs of disgust rather than approval. To his eyes, men beaten while bound and unable to defend themselves, was not justice.

Phillip also hoped the floggings would convince the troublemakers that the natives must not be disturbed. After the convicts' bad conduct, he had to begin again trying to build trust with the natives.

However something terrible happened in early April 1789, to make any good result seem impossible. Watkin Tench called the tragedy that hit the native people 'an extraordinary calamity'.

Dead bodies, and lots of them, were seen around the harbour, on the beaches and in rock shelters. Upon examining the corpses, Surgeon John White believed the cause of death was smallpox, a virus causing fever and painful pus-filled blisters to cover the body. It was a mystery how and where the disease came from, as only native people had died. None of the white population was affected. Governor Phillip sent parties of men down the harbour to search for survivors. If they could treat the victims, their concern and kindness would prove their good wishes. But all they found were bodies.

Then in mid-April a marine who had been gathering building material for Lieutenant Johnston, came rushing into the settlement with news that natives were in distress in a nearby cove. They were very sick, but at least they were still alive. The Governor, with John White the Chief Surgeon and Arabanoo hurried to the spot.

They found an elderly man beside a small fire suffering from high fever, and a boy pouring water from a shell onto the man's forehead. A little girl lay dead nearby. They felt choked by the dedication of the little boy to the older man and the miserable condition of them both. Watkin Tench wrote about it in his journal.

Eruptions covered the poor boy from head to foot, and the old man was so weak it was difficult to get him to the boat. Their condition made it impossible for them to struggle, and they quietly submitted to be carried away.

Arabanoo seemed unwilling to approach them at first, but his shyness soon wore off, and he treated them with kind attention.

Arabanoo did not want to leave the site until he buried the child's body. He scooped a grave in the sand with his hands then lined the hole completely with grass, before putting the little girl's body into it. Finally he made a raised mound with earth above the grave.

The little boy and the older man were taken to the hospital at Sydney Cove, where they were kept separate from the other patients. Arabanoo insisted on staying with them and treated them with tenderness. He told them they need not be afraid of the white men.

'Budyeree,' (good) he told the sick man. 'Good men here.'

The sick man nodded, and looked toward the little boy. The words gave him comfort; they eased his mind.

'Bado, bado,' (Water, water) the sick man called in a hoarse voice.

Arabanoo tried to help by trickling water gently down his swollen throat. He knew he was dying in the territory of the white people and it was a comfort to have black hands gently lifting water to his lips. Watkin Tench saw the relief in both patients' eyes.

> *By the encouragement of Arabanoo, who assured them of our protection, and the soothing manners of our medical gentlemen, they became settled, and looked grateful for their situation.*

However, sickness and hunger had exhausted the older man so much he was not expected to recover. He lived only a few more hours, fading away without a sound. The young boy handled the moment of the older man's death with quiet acceptance.

'Boee,' (dead) the child said simply, looking toward the man.

'The tenderness and concern of the older man for the boy was very moving,' Watkin Tench said later, talking with the doctor.

'The poor man could hardly lift his head but while he had strength, he kept looking at the boy and patting him gently. Then with dying eyes, he seemed to give his child into our care and protection.'

After consulting with Arabanoo, the man was buried. The Governor and his officers attended a brief ceremony for him. That day Phillip decided that Arabanoo must have his freedom again.

'After everything that's happened, we have to trust that he knows we want to help him and his people. It's clear he has great affection for them and he seems to have confidence in us now.'

He went to talk to Arabanoo and with the few words they shared he spoke his thoughts as the man's restraint was removed.

'Arabanoo, I hope you will stay in Sydney Cove,' the Governor said slowly. Arabanoo nodded.

'U-ry-di-ow,' (Stay near) The Governor thought he understood what Arabanoo meant. He nodded to show he was pleased.

Arabanoo did stay. He had seen the white people's puzzling ways. They ate strange food and used strange objects. He didn't understand why they were there, or how they had come to his land. Maybe they had lost their way. He could see the white leader meant well but he needed to learn a lot of things. His own people were gone it seemed, so he decided to stay at Sydney Cove.

****

Nanberry, the little boy aged about nine, recovered from his illness and was adopted by the doctor who'd saved his life. A close bond had already grown between them, and it was clear to anyone seeing them together, that the little boy was very attached to John White.

'You can tell me about the birds and animals, and the plants that grow around Sydney Cove,' he said to the boy, seeing his lost expression after leaving the hospital. 'And you can call me father.'

The boy nodded, understanding the main words. He knew 'father' meant the same as 'be-anna'. His be-anna had gone now. He wanted to help the man who looked after him. He could show him which plants were medicine, which were good to eat and which were not. It was puzzling that 'father' didn't already know all about the healing plants. Maybe the white men used different medicine because they came from a faraway place.

Nanberry knew John White was called 'doctor' or 'surgeon' by the white people, and that meant he was a very important man in Sydney Cove. He was like a *Koradji,* a healing man among his own people. Thinking about his people made him sad. He would try to think about other things.

He was learning English words quickly by listening to conversations at the hospital, and between the doctor and the officers. He also asked lots of questions.

'What is this father?' He asked pointing to one of the things he wore.

'That's your jacket,' said John White, pleased at the boy's interest.

Nanberry thought as they walked around, that the 'jackets' on the people in Sydney Cove had different meanings and he wanted to know why. John White saw him looking at the people around him and guessed his question.

'The Governor wears a '*blue* jacket' and Lieutenant Tench wears a '*red* jacket', because of their jobs,' he explained.

Then seeing Nanberry's confusion, he added. 'You will understand with time, lad.'

'Can I wear a blue jacket, father?' Nanberry asked.

'Yes, I will get a blue jacket made for you,' John White said smiling.

Doctor White looked at the bright little boy trying to take everything in, and he felt a flicker of something close to happiness. He was so thankful the boy had lived. Since leaving England, he'd been surrounded by nothing but sickness and death. He had servants, but no wife or children and he was lonely. This boy had brought new joy to his life.

****

But John White could not escape sickness and death. The smallpox epidemic had not run its course. It continued to take victims among the black population around the harbour. When the white men went in boats to look for more survivors, Arabanoo went with them hoping to find some of his companions alive. After a day searching, George Johnston told Esther how helpless and sorry he felt for him.

'I'll never forget Arabanoo's grief and pain as he looked around the different bays we visited. There were no signs of life, not a living person anywhere, not even footprints in the sand.'

'Oh George, that's terrible.' Esther felt tears sting her eyes.

During the following day they found rotting bodies in the caves above another beach. After taking in the scene, Arabanoo raised his hands in silent agony and stood there a long time.

'Dead! All dead!' he cried. Then he hung his head in grief, not saying another word for the rest of the journey.

A day later two sick natives, a young man and his fourteen-year-old sister, were found in a very bad way and brought into Sydney Cove. Arabanoo treated them with great care and Doctor White did everything he could, but the young man died within three days. When the girl, whose name was Boorong, saw he was dying she crept to his side and lay beside him till his life silently slipped away.

****

When her health improved, Boorong went to live in the household of Reverend Johnson and his wife, Mary. They saw it as a wonderful opportunity to teach the young girl about Christianity and the benefits of a British lifestyle. They tried to make her feel welcome and she sensed their kind feelings toward her. Elizabeth Hayward didn't know what to think when Boorong came to live with them.

'The Reverend makes a big fuss of her,' she told Susannah Kable. 'He's teaching her the Lord's Prayer and says she's learnin' words real quick.'

'Well you could help her too, by telling her the words she needs,' Susannah suggested. 'You could show her things when you finish your jobs. She must be feeling a bit out of place, poor girl.'

'Well I didn't 'ave anyone to show me 'round, did I?' Elizabeth blurted, knowing it wasn't a kind thing to say. Susannah gave her a warning look, reminding Elizabeth of the beating she'd received weeks before. A public beating at that! She'd said things to the Reverend that she knew she shouldn't say and had received 'thirty lashes for insolence'. She hadn't understood the word before but now she knew 'insolence' meant 'being cheeky'.

'Yes, I'll 'ave to watch me tongue,' Elizabeth said, remembering her painful back, her tears and hurt pride.

****

Elizabeth's back was still sore a week later at the christening of Isabella Rawson's baby. That day however, as she watched the Reverend blessing the child, her tears were happy ones, at seeing Isabella with a healthy baby in her arms.

The tiny boy was named Joseph after his father, a marine who wouldn't see his son grow because he planned to return to England.

'Don't worry about Isabella,' Susannah Kable said when Elizabeth showed concern. 'She'll be fine. That nice man, William Richardson has asked her to marry 'im, and Isabella's said yes!'

****

In the meantime the native girl Boorong was adjusting to life at Sydney Cove. At fourteen she was a bright, light-hearted girl who loved playing, singing, and generally having fun. She soon realised that noisy laughter was not the usual way in the Reverend Johnson's household. They smiled kindly, but they didn't laugh out loud often. It wasn't like the family life she remembered around the campfires.

However, it became clear to her that like Nanberry, she lived in the home of an important man. 'Reverend' was a special name, similar to a man of special power among her own people. She could see it pleased the Reverend when she repeated the important words he called 'Lord's Prayer', so she did her best to remember them. She could see he wanted to help her. She felt welcome in Sydney Cove, but she felt lost. The Ma'am was very quiet and the girl Elizabeth watched her a lot. They tried to talk but there was not much to say.

There were things in Sydney Cove Boorong found difficult. The food was strange. She missed eating sweet, sticky yams, warm from the fire. She missed collecting wigi berries by the basketful with her friends and gobbling them till her belly ached.

And there were the body coverings the white people called 'clothes'. These consisted of many parts, some for men and some for women. She tried to remember the names. She must wear a 'petticoat' and a 'skirt'. On her feet she wore 'shoes', and on her head she wore a 'hat'. She was surprised to learn that she had to wear clothes *all the time*, even when swimming and sleeping.

She missed sitting around the campfire at night and sleeping under the stars. It was airless and smelt strange inside the Reverend's shelter. She missed being on the water in her canoe and singing with the other girls as they paddled around the headlands. They always sang.

She hummed a familiar song and it reminded her of fishing with her friends who were now gone. She didn't want to forget the songs of her people. Maybe she'd teach Elizabeth her songs. She would see.

****

In the meantime, Arabanoo continued to teach and learn from the white people and to enjoy their friendship. In early May, he met another of the Governor's officers for the first time. Captain John Hunter had returned to Sydney Cove from his seven-month voyage to Africa to buy food for the colony. On arriving, he visited the Governor to give his report. He was surprised to see an unfamiliar man in the Governor's sitting room, and he wrote about it:

> *As soon as the ship was secured, I went ashore to see the governor. He was sitting by the fire, drinking tea with a few friends among whom I observed a native man, who was well clothed and seemed to be as much at ease at the tea-table as any person there. He managed his cup and saucer as if he'd been used to doing it a long time.*

Not long after that happy afternoon, something terrible happened to bring Arabanoo's time in Sydney Cove to a tragic end. He caught smallpox himself and died in mid-May, eight days after his symptoms began.

When he became sick, everything possible was done to stop his suffering and save his life. Watkin Tench grieved his death, but he believed Arabanoo knew they'd tried their best for him. He'd chosen to stay in Sydney Cove after he was free to leave. Tench wrote about Arabanoo's final days in his journal.

> *During his sickness he had complete confidence in us. Although a stranger to our medicine, and hating the taste of it, he swallowed all the drugs the doctor gave him in the hope of them helping him.*
>
> *The governor, who particularly regarded him, arranged for him to be buried in his own garden.*

Governor Phillip was deeply saddened by the loss of Arabanoo. He had grown to admire the man for his kind-hearted nature and quiet self-control. He'd taught them many things about his culture, but there was so much more they needed to know. The little boy Nanberry, and the girl Boorong in her early teens, were now the only natives living in the British settlement. The Governor needed to re-think his plan for building a relationship with the native people after the terrible loss and damage smallpox had caused.

****

The Aboriginal people also had to consider ways of adjusting to their weakened situation. Their numbers had been greatly reduced by the smallpox epidemic they called 'gal-galla'. Family groups would have to band together, in order to survive.

Chapter 22

Sydney Cove, June - August 1789

Winter brought cold nights and frosty mornings but the settlers knew what to expect; it was the second year in their new home.

Life in Sydney Cove had become more familiar, however they were anxious about the lack of communication from England. It had been two years since they'd left on their voyage to this land. They'd heard nothing in all that time from their families and friends. They knew there was nothing they could do about it, but watch and wait for a ship to arrive.

At least they could look forward to some cheer on June 4th. For weeks planning had been going on for the King's Birthday celebrations. This year as well as the military parade and cannons firing, there would be an extra treat in the evening. A group of convicts had asked the Governor's approval to put on a performance. It was a play called 'The Recruiting Officer'.

'I can't believe we're actually puttin' on a show,' said Susannah unable to hide her excitement. 'It's 'ard to believe, in't it Henry?'

In their spare time, the convicts practised their lines and prepared a platform in one of the cabbage tree huts as a stage and opened one of the sides so an audience could watch from outside. They had used whatever they could for decoration: strips of paper, branches from trees and things the women had sewn together.

'What's a recruiting officer?' Elizabeth Hayward wanted to know.
'And what's the play all about?' She was intrigued with the idea.

'Well, recruiting officers 'ave to get people to join the military. That's their job,' Old Dot told her. 'The Recruitin' Officer' was a stage play in London when I was a girl. Famous it was.'

'But what's it all about?' Elizabeth asked again.

'As far I remember, it's about two officers in competition for the same lass. You know, the usual stuff,' Dot nodded and winked. 'There's a bit o' romance 'n lots of funny bits too.'

'Did you know His Excellency said he'd come along an' the officers too?' Elizabeth passed on the gossip but didn't believe it herself.

'Ay, His Excellency's alright I reckon. He lets me off from workin' due to me old age. I reckon 'is heart's in the right place.'

Elizabeth smiled to herself. Dorothy Handland swore she was over eighty-two, but most people believed she was younger. It was her haggard face and rotten teeth that made her look ancient. But Old Dot as she called herself, used it to her advantage.

****

Watkin Tench saw rehearsals going on for the play and decided he'd like to see it. He asked Lieutenant William Dawes about going too.

'It'll add a bit of excitement to the place. It's very dull here most of the time. What do you say, Dawes?'

'I have work to do at the observatory, but I may come for a while.'

Watkin Tench liked William Dawes a lot. He was intelligent and thoughtful, but he was very serious at times.

'I've heard there'll be some jokes thrown in about our situation here. I hope the convicts know which officers can take a joke.'

****

Governor Phillip did attend the performance and laughed along with the rest of the audience which consisted of marines and convicts.

Watkin Tench was there and told William Dawes all about it.

'I'm not ashamed to say I laughed till my sides ached. The actors were brilliant and from the clapping, I think everyone including the Governor enjoyed the jokes the convict threw in about our strange setting here on the edge of the world.'

For Governor Phillip, June 4th 1789 had been a memorable day. He'd dined with his officers earlier in the day in his newly completed residence. He was living in a proper house at last. With things more settled at Sydney Cove, it was time for more exploring.

****

With a settlement now at Rose Hill, the Governor hoped the mysterious 'blue mountains' would be easier to reach. However, he knew from experience that discovering a route westward, and over the mountains, would not be as simple as it appeared.

During the winter of 1789, the Governor, along with George Johnston, John White and others, headed north-west. They found a wide twisting river later named the 'Hawkesbury'. On its banks they saw places where yams and other root vegetables had been dug up, but the food gatherers were no-where in sight. They saw no-one until one day they came upon a young woman hiding in the long grass only a few steps from their tent site. They only discovered her there when she squealed loudly at the sound of gun blast as the men shot a bird for their dinner.

When the men approached her, she was crying and shaking in fear. The girl began calling toward the forest but no one replied. The British men didn't understand her words but could see her panic.

'She looks like she's seen a ghost, poor girl. Clearly, she couldn't get away when we arrived because she's ill, so she's hidden here.'

The Governor ordered his men to get her water, make a fire, and cook the skinned birds that had just been shot.

'It looks like she's had smallpox,' said Doctor John White. 'She'll survive I think - if she gets over this shock.'

'Bado?' the Governor offered her water using a word he'd learnt from Arabanoo. Hearing a familiar word seemed to calm the girl.

She drank the water and ate the roasted birds and the men left her with bundles of dried grass to pile around herself for warmth.

The following morning they left their campsite to continue their exploration. They knew the girl's companions were nearby because she'd kept calling to them, but it was not until the men returned to their boat that they saw natives come out of the forest.

The explorers continued surveying the river system but returned to Sydney without reaching the mountains, when supplies ran out.

****

At the end of June, Watkin Tench set off with another exploring party hoping to reach new territory. They left Rose Hill at daybreak and headed toward the mountains. On their second day out they found themselves in a quiet valley, on the banks of a wide river. Tench wrote in his diary:

> *Vast flocks of wild ducks were swimming in the river but after being once fired at, they grew so shy that we could not get near them a second time. Nothing is more certain than that the sound of a gun had never before been heard at this spot.*

While exploring the area they saw canoes, huts, animal and bird traps, but no people. They returned to Sydney to report their finds to the Governor: a wide river and good farming land, but they hadn't met any people. Due to supplies running low, they hadn't ventured *into* the mountains but they'd been close to the foothills.

****

All through the white men's journey, the natives had remained at a safe distance. They'd heard the white men's shouts of delight on seeing the wide river with its huge flock of ducks. When one of the strangers pointed his 'firestick' at the ducks and sent them flying off, the natives had looked at each other with puzzled expressions.

Wasn't it obvious that such a noise would send the birds away? Didn't they know there were simpler ways to snare a water bird?

They watched the white men inspecting and discussing the axe marks cut into tree trunks. They were the footholds the natives used to climb to higher branches to collect honey, birds' eggs, and pounce on sleeping possums. They saw the white men examining their bird traps of crisscrossed branches and reeds, cleverly placed along the riverbank. And although they couldn't understand the white men's words, they saw the admiration in their expressions. They watched the men look into their empty bark dwellings and then scan the surrounding area with baffled expressions.

Where are the people?

Once again, in the wilderness, it had been easy for the natives to observe the white men while staying unnoticed themselves.

Chapter 23

Sydney Cove, September - December 1789

Warmer weather arrived, and for Nanberry and Boorong that meant a time for gathering nectar-filled flowers to soak for a delicious sweet drink. It was a time for collecting figs and berries, and eating their fill. They noticed there weren't as many bushes as last season, but they didn't worry. There was bread and rice at the Sydney Cove.

Little did they realise that the Governor was worried. He had decided to cut food rations in the settlement by a third. He was concerned that if ships didn't arrive from England soon, they would run out of supplies of flour, rice and salted meat. They had only brought two years supply from England and that time was nearly up.

The Governor had other things on his mind too. Months had passed since the death of Arabanoo and he was unsure how to move forward with the natives around Sydney Cove. By the end of 1789, he had made a decision. This time Lieutenant Bradley received the order to kidnap more natives, and he was not happy about it.

William Bradley thought about the native men he was about to capture; they would have families that would miss them. He had been away from his own wife in England for so long that he knew what separation was like. He felt strongly about family ties.

But orders were orders. An officer wouldn't dare disobey a command from his Governor, so Bradley set off across the harbour.

He wrote a gripping account of what happened that day:

November, 1789

As we went down the harbour we caught some fish. Seeing a great number of natives on a beach, we headed to them.

As we got near we held up two large fish and had the good luck to draw two men away from the group. The men came around the rocks where they left their spears and met us on the beach near the boat, far enough from the others to promise success without losing any lives. They eagerly took the fish.

Four of the crew were kept in the boat which was backed close to the beach where the two natives stood. They were dancing together when the signal was given by me and the poor devils were seized and handed into the boat in an instant.

The natives on the beach saw us seize them, and ran with their spears but we were too quick for them. We pulled out immediately without having to fire a shot.

The noise of the men, the crying and screaming of the women and children, together with the situation of the two miserable wretches in our possession was really a most distressing scene. They were terrified and kept calling out to those on the shore.

The troubled young Lieutenant Bradley later told his friends.

'It was by far the most unpleasant service I was ever ordered to do.'

Like others with family in England, William Bradley was homesick. Seeing the native men's panic and the distress in their eyes at being taken from their people, he regretted his part in the kidnap plot.

When Bradley and his crew landed at Sydney Cove with their captives, the scene was similar to the arrival of Arabanoo. Crowds of curious onlookers gathered at the wharf.

'Colbee! Bennelong!' Nanberry called excitedly when he saw them. He couldn't believe his eyes.

He had often talked proudly about his Uncle Colbee to John White. He hadn't known if any of his family had survived smallpox but now he knew at least Colbee was alive. He told everyone in the crowd:

'Colbee is a great warrior and leading man of my people,' he called running after the men, but the captives kept their heads down.

Lieutenant Bradley led the men from the wharf to the Governor's house where Boorong, the native girl, also recognised them and called their names. She was thrilled to see them, but the native men were in no mood for a reunion. They were weighed down with leg irons and tied with ropes. They were angry.

The Governor tried to speak to them using words he'd learnt from Arabanoo, but the men did not answer him. He then asked the native children, Boorong and Nanberry, to tell the men they'd be safe and well treated, and later would be free to return to their friends. He gave orders for them to be made comfortable but guarded closely in a small hut beside his own house.

Feeling for them, Lieutenant Bradley wanted to know if the men had families who would be distressed about their capture. Nanberry told him neither man had a wife, and the information eased the marine's mind.

The native men were shaved, washed and clothed but the whole time they were gloomy. It didn't improve matters when an iron shackle was again put on each man's leg with a rope tied to it and a convict put in charge of watching them. That night William Bradley wondered how the prisoners were coping, hemmed behind four walls and a locked door. They were in fact already working on their escape plan. Despite the iron shackles, the rope and the guards, the men tried to escape by biting through the ropes while their guards were asleep. It did not succeed at first, but Colbee, determined to have his freedom, escaped a week later.

Bennelong was now the sole captive and became more afraid. Aware that the guard was flogged for allowing Colbee's escape, he expected it would also happen to him. However, the Governor assured him it would not, and he soon realised he had a special role at Sydney Cove. He was there to teach the white people about his culture. Within a short time, he settled into his new position and readily told the Governor about his people, his customs and his country.

It was clear to the Governor that Bennelong was intelligent and motivated. He quickly learnt the habits and manners he saw around him and seemed to enjoy wearing British clothes. He ate at the Governor's table and soon knew enough English words to have a simple conversation. He had a huge appetite and happily tried the wine offered by the officers. When the British raised their glasses, nodded their heads and called 'The King!' he was quick to do the same.

Bennelong was very different to Arabanoo who had been a quiet, thoughtful man. Bennelong, on the other hand, loved talking, joking and boasting about himself and the battles he'd won.

'Love and war seem to be his favourite topics and he has the scars to prove it,' Watkin Tench said as a group sat talking.

Bennelong, understanding the gist of the conversation, pointed to the scars on his head. He showed them where a spear had passed through his arm and another through his leg. Half of one thumb was missing and he had a bad wound on the back of his hand.

'The scar on your hand Bennelong, how did you get it?' the officers asked. Bennelong laughed, saying he'd received it from a woman.

'She bit my hand,' he said, demonstrating to make sure they got his meaning. Fascinated by his tales, the officers encouraged him with more questions.

'What about your other scars, Bennelong? Tell us about them.'

And he would stand, holding his spear to demonstrate what happened in each case, raising his voice as he relived all the details of battles fought with other warriors.

It was very clear that Bennelong loved being the centre of attention and the officers certainly enjoyed his energy. He was also a very fast learner.

It wasn't long before Bennelong noticed that people in Sydney Cove had different levels of importance. He noted that they showed their position by their clothes, so he was keen to wear the outfit of a gentleman. At other times, he wore a red jacket an officer had given to him.

'He seems to be impressed with everything he sees,' Phillip told George Johnston. 'He said he will call me Be-anna, which has the same meaning as 'father'. It's a good sign that he's so relaxed and comfortable with us.'

'Yes, he doesn't lack confidence,' replied Lieutenant Johnston. 'And I think we will learn a lot from him. He's very intelligent.'

****

Bennelong was soon in the Governor's boat with officers crossing the harbour. He was keen to show them places of importance to him. He pointed to an island the Governor had named Goat Island.

'Me-mel,' Bennelong told them was the island's original name. 'My place,' he explained. It had been his father's property, but now it was *his* island.

He showed them places with rock art and tried to explain their meanings to the white men. Some images he said were there to teach the children about hunting and the laws of his people. It was an education for the white men.

****

While the Governor was learning more about the environment of Sydney Cove from Bennelong, he sent Lieutenants George Johnston and William Dawes on a mission to find a way across the mountains. Their group set off on foot in mid-December with high hopes of achieving their goal. They knew the dangers of going where no white man had been before. There was no way of getting help if something went wrong in one of the deep canyons of the wilderness region, but they needed to know what was out there.

This time at least the explorers did travel some distance into the mountain range. For days they climbed up and down sandstone gorges, only to see more of the same ahead of them. The country was so rugged they finally gave up in exhaustion, returning to Sydney a week later.

The most useful result of the journey was a map Dawes made of the area they'd covered. As the men looked over the chart with the Governor, it highlighted their isolation. The colony was a dot on the edge of an immense wilderness area that sat on the rim of a lonely ocean, about as far from the known world as they could get.

Chapter 24

Sydney Cove, January - February 1790

By the beginning of 1790, the settlers were becoming more anxious and impatient for news from England. They felt cut off from the world. Besides that, they were running out of supplies.

At Rose Hill, the settlement was progressing but they hadn't produced enough grain to make flour for the colony. James Ruse, by now a free man, was working hard on his project but he needed more time to get his farm going. And it wasn't only food the colony needed; it was candles, paper and cloth, rope and leather for mending shoes and many other things.

Trouble was taken to hide the colony's worsening food shortage from Bennelong. He had a huge appetite and extra fish was included in his diet whenever possible.

'I don't want him to know about our alarming situation,' Governor Phillip said to George Johnston. 'If he passes the information on to his people, they could take advantage of our weakened state. He mustn't have any idea of our terrible position.'

'I agree completely,' replied Johnston. 'He was brought into the settlement to show him the benefits of our society. We don't want him to think this is how civilised people usually live. I agree, he must not see our distress.'

Meanwhile, as Bennelong continued observing the ways of the white people, they watched as he demonstrated valuable bush skills to them.

They gathered around as he told them how his people created fire. The Governor's secretary wrote the process in his journal:

> *It is made by fixing the pointed end of a cylindrical piece of wood into a hollow made in a flat piece. The operator twirls the round piece swiftly between both his hands, sliding them up and down as long as he can, at which time another of his companions takes over. They sit for this purpose in a circle, and each one takes his turn until fire is produced.*

Nanberry was there when Bennelong shared the skills of his people, and it brought back memories of his father. He remembered being in the forest with him, especially the day his father passed on the art of fire making. Nanberry thought a lot about the life he'd had with his people.

One day he wanted to be a warrior like his father so he would ask Bennelong to help him practise the skills he would need. He didn't want to forget the ways of his people.

He thought about his new life with the white people. They had many good things. He enjoyed being with his adopted father, roaming the forests with him. On exploring trips, John White asked Nanberry questions, praising and making him feel important when he spotted and pointed out birds, insects, lizards and snakes.

Most of all, Nanberry loved being on the harbour with John White.

The English men caught many fish in their nets at one time and their boats were very big. One day, Nanberry thought, he would like to go beyond the harbour, on a long journey in one of the white people's ships. He decided that after he'd become a warrior, he would sail across the ocean.

****

While an exchange of information and experiences continued between the different cultures, two convicts, Isabella Rawson and William Richardson were busy making plans. They believed the children of Sydney Cove also needed an education.

Isabella had married William in the springtime and she was happier than she'd ever been. They shared the same vision for teaching the little ones. They both wanted to give the children of convicts the best possible chance of improving their lives.

Seven years earlier William Richardson had been sentenced to hang for stealing, but his penalty was changed to transportation. When the First Fleet arrived in Sydney Cove, he'd been assigned as a servant to an officer because he could read and write.

Now he and Isabella were going to set up the first school in the colony with the Reverend Johnson's backing. As the minister handed them books he'd brought from England, he gave them his blessing.

'Give these out to those who appear most deserving,' he told them.

'When ships finally arrive, I will write for more to be sent.'

That night the Reverend told his wife Mary how happy he was that some good was being done for the little ones.

'Improvement must begin with the rising generation,' he said.

'Yes dear,' she replied, thinking about the children of Sydney Cove and what the future held for them.

Mary Johnson was expecting a baby again, and because her first had not lived, she was nervous about the coming birth…and afterward. She kept her anxious thoughts to herself, but she was worried about their situation. Her husband worked hard in their little garden so they always had a supply of vegetables. But what about clothes, shoes and blankets? They needed those too.

'Our own little one will be here soon,' her husband said, reading her thoughts. 'We must trust in the Lord,' he added in a calm tone. 'Don't worry dear, a ship will arrive from England soon, I'm sure.'

****

When Boorong and Elizabeth learnt there was going to be a baby in their household, they eagerly offered names for the little one.

'I like Maria for a girl,' Elizabeth said, pleased to give her opinion. 'Milbah,' suggested Boorong brightly. 'It's a girl's name among my people.'

'Well we shall have to wait and see what the Lord sends us,' said Mary Johnson, happy that the girls had a common interest.

Boorong had lived in Sydney Cove for almost a year and felt more settled. She had adjusted to English food and the Reverend encouraged her to collect berries, and other bush food growing near the settlement to include in their household diet.

'But don't go too far Boorong,' Mrs Johnson always gently advised.

'Yes Ma'am,' Boorong called over her shoulder.

She loved spending time walking through bushland near the water, away from the bustle.

****

One late summer afternoon she stood looking out across the bay at pelicans gliding above. She was whispering a song of her people when she saw Elizabeth Hayward walking by, carrying a bucket.

'Look,' she called, 'Car-rang-a bo mur-ray.'

'What does that mean?' Elizabeth asked as she approached.

'Big water bird,' Boorong replied, pointing.

'We say pelican,' said Elizabeth pleased she could teach Boorong.

'Yes,' Boorong nodded. 'When we see a pelican in the sky,
we sing a special song: **'Gnoo-roo-me, tatie, natie natie,**
Gnoo-roo-me, tatie, natie natie,
Tarrah wow, tarrah wow...'

Elizabeth repeated the words in her head and then tried to say them the way Boorong did.

'Good, budyeree,' Boorong praised her in English and her language.

Elizabeth felt her face redden. She smiled and turned to leave.

'Wait, look!' Boorong shouted excitedly. 'There, in the water, there.' She pointed to dolphins leaping out of the bay.

'We have a song for this too,' she said with a bright smile.

Seeing Elizabeth put her bucket down, she explained the sequence, using gestures as she sang the words slowly.

'When the fish is above water, we sing: **No-te-le-bre-la-la,'**
'When it goes under the sea, we sing: **No-tee No-tee**, till it rises.'

Elizabeth repeated the words and Boorong nodded her approval.

'Learning new songs is easier than learning to write letters,' she giggled as she walked down the hill singing to herself.

Chapter 25

Sydney Cove, March 1790

By March, the people of Sydney Cove were becoming desperate. Since they'd arrived and set up their remote campsite, they hadn't heard a word from their families, their friends, or their government. Everyone was becoming weary and dejected. In all that time – more than two long years – there hadn't been a single follow-up ship with supplies from Britain. Yet every day they still hoped and expected one may arrive. At the sound of distant thunder, or the echo of a hunter's gunshot, people would stop and listen expectantly.

What was that? Could it be a ship's gun firing as a signal?

And they would go racing to the headland to search the ocean, hoping and praying there would be a sail. But it was nothing...again, and they would turn and walk back down the hill to the settlement.

The supplies brought with them from England had become dangerously low. When women chatted as they worked, when convicts carted bricks or dragged logs together, when marines met on the parade ground, they all talked about the same thing.

When will ships arrive with supplies?
What's going on? Have we been abandoned?
How much longer can we survive like this?

They desperately needed basics like flour and rice, but they also missed luxuries like tea, salt and sugar. And they needed tools to replace those lost and damaged.

Doctor White, caring for sick convicts and marines at the hospital, was anxious about dwindling medical supplies. He felt frustrated and angry when he put into words what others were thinking:

'In the name of heaven, what is our government doing? Surely they have quite forgotten or neglected us...Lord have mercy on us!'

The waiting was getting to everyone. There were endless discussions about what could have happened to the long-awaited ships.

What if ships have come, but couldn't find us?
What if they sailed straight past the entrance to the harbour?

As added insurance, the Governor directed that a lookout be set up on a high bluff at the harbour's entrance. If a ship appeared on the horizon, a flag would be raised to alert the ship of the colony's whereabouts. From daylight till the sun went down, a sentry swept the distant ocean with his telescope in the hope of seeing a sail.

Governor Phillip knew he'd soon have to reduce everyone's rations again. As a step to ease the situation, he decided to send some convicts and marines to Norfolk Island. He hoped that by dividing the population over two settlements, their chance of survival would increase. The two government ships, *HMS Sirius* and *HMS Supply*, would take them to the little island where the first settlers had been sent two years earlier. They'd shown success in growing food there, so it made sense to send more people now.

Among the convicts heading to Norfolk Island, were the two youngest, John Hudson and Elizabeth Hayward. Like everyone going, they had mixed feelings about the move. They were told it was for their own good, but they were leaving dear friends, and a place they'd begun to think of as home.

John Hudson didn't understand the food crisis everyone talked about.

The native people had lived in this place long before them, and they'd survived. But he was just a young lad and nobody asked his opinion, so he kept it to himself. When the time came for goodbyes, James Ruse put his hand on John's thin shoulder.

'Now lad, stay out of trouble,' he said. 'Maybe we'll meet again.'
'Ay,' John replied. He wanted to say more, but didn't know what.

For Elizabeth, the parting was much harder than she showed. Mary Johnson had given birth to a baby girl she called Milbah Maria, two days before the ships sailed. Elizabeth realised she would miss the Ma'am, and even the Reverend, despite his scolding. She knew he had her welfare at heart. She didn't want to leave their household now, but she had no choice. The Governor had decided.

'Remember the things we've taught you Lizzie,' said the Reverend. 'Keep learning your letters and don't forget to say your prayers.'
Elizabeth just nodded. She couldn't find the right words to reply.

'I won't forget the songs you taught me,' she said to Boorong.

'And I won't forget your cheek,' said Old Dot looking older than ever.

After tearful farewells, the passengers boarded and set sail on March 6th 1790 to face another beginning, in another new place.

****

Also sailing to Norfolk Island for a short-term posting was Lieutenant George Johnston and with him went Esther Abrahams and her daughter Roseanna, as well as their newborn baby, George. Esther was pleased that she was now known publicly as George Johnston's partner. She was also relieved to be leaving the Sydney settlement during its terrible food shortage. On Norfolk Island, she'd heard, there were better farming conditions and fewer mouths to feed. Little did they know the disaster that lay ahead.

The plan was for *HMS Sirius* to continue on to China to purchase supplies for the colony, after delivering the settlers to Norfolk Island.

****

With the departure of the ships for Norfolk Island the Governor watched the food store at Sydney Cove drop to its lowest level. He hoped a ship would arrive from England before announcing another ration cut. He made it known he had exactly the same food allowance as everyone else in the colony, but that didn't stop the grumbling. Everyone's quota was cut to a little more than half a cup of rice, half a cup of flour and a similar amount of dried meat each day. The food had come from England. It was very stale and crawling with little bugs, called weevils. Tench recorded the details:

> *The pork had been salted between three and four years ago and every grain of rice was a moving body, from the insects crawling within it.*
>
> *We stopped boiling the pork as it had become so old and dry, that it shrunk one half in its size. Our method of cooking it was to cut a slice, and toast it on a fork before the fire, catching the drops which fell on a slice of bread, or in a saucer of rice.*

The ration was enough to keep them alive, but only for so long, and only if fresh food was added. Winter would soon be on them which meant less fish in the harbour. Things became so bad that the Governor reduced the working hours because nobody had the strength to do physical labour for more than a few hours a day.

Added to this serious situation was the fact that most of the settlers' clothes were in tatters and their blankets had worn thin.

Even the guards paraded with holes in their faded jackets and some patrolled the settlement without shoes. The division between the classes of people at Sydney Cove had become blurred – officers, marines and convicts were all in the same situation. They all wore threadbare clothes. They all felt desperate.

Households like the Kables and the Reverend's were coping better than most because they'd kept up their vegetable gardens, but these were constantly being robbed in the night.

'If only more of the lazy so-and-sos around here would grow their own stuff, we may not be in this trouble,' Henry growled.

'Ay,' Susannah agreed. 'More peas disappeared overnight, and we can't blame the possums.'

In a move to deter food thieves, the punishment for stealing was increased. The Governor issued a statement:

'Anyone caught robbing from a garden will receive three hundred lashes immediately. They will be chained for six months and have their ration of flour cut for the same period.'

The thieving stopped for a while, but the mood in the colony was bleak. All hope for its survival was pinned on *HMS Sirius* returning with supplies from China before their stores totally ran out.

If they had known about the calamity that was happening off Norfolk Island, they may have given up in despair. But they continued holding on to a glimmer of hope, believing relief was on its way. That is, until unexpected news arrived.

****

The flag on the headland was up to signal that a ship had been sighted. It should have caused a great stir of excitement but something didn't seem right. Watkin Tench raced down to Dawes' observatory and peered through the large telescope toward the sentry post on the headland. He saw immediately something was wrong. A lone guard strolled back and forth. There was no excitement in his step.

What is going on?

Tench hurried back to the main settlement to find the Governor about to be rowed down the harbour to investigate.

'May I accompany you sir?' he pleaded.

'Yes, yes, but hurry man,' the Governor appeared anxious.

Halfway to the harbour's entrance, they saw a rowboat belonging to *HMS Supply* approaching. As it came nearer, Tench saw one of the seamen make a gesture that told them plainly that something disastrous had happened.

'Sir, I think we should prepare ourselves for bad news,' Tench said turning to his superior. Governor Phillip looked pale.

They soon learnt that *HMS Sirius* had been shipwrecked off Norfolk Island. No supplies would be coming from China anytime soon. It was an unbelievable disaster, but at least everyone on board had managed to get safely ashore on the island before weather conditions changed. The ship had then struck hidden rocks of a reef near the shore, and began taking water into its hold. *HMS Sirius* could not be saved.

The wreck of *HMS Sirius* off Norfolk Island, 1790

Chapter 26

Sydney Cove, April - May 1790

With news of the *Sirius* wreck, the Governor called an emergency meeting with his officers in Sydney Cove. Drastic measures were necessary and he needed their support. They somehow had to make their supplies last and pray that a ship would arrive soon from England. The Reverend Johnson described their situation in a letter he hoped to send one day to his friend in England:

Dear friend,

It is now a long, long time since I have been able to write or hear from you. I am happy to inform you we are still alive, but have had many ups & downs.

It is now about two years and three months since we first arrived in this distant country. All this while, we have been as if buried alive, never having an opportunity of hearing from our friends.

Our stock of supplies brought from England, is nearly gone. We have been anxiously looking out for a fleet for a long time, but so far none has appeared, and we now imagine the fleet we expected is either lost or taken by some enemy. Our hopes now are almost vanished, and every one begins to think our situation very alarming.

Richard Johnson, April 9th, 1790.

The terrible conditions in the colony made some residents begin thinking about escape. Certain ones had definite plans for leaving.

****

All through their period of hunger and concern, the Governor had tried to hide from Bennelong the fact that the colony was on the edge of starvation. But he was an intelligent man and he wasn't blind, so no matter how the officers tried to mislead and distract him, Bennelong could not miss the state of the colony. Besides he was missing his people.

Bennelong decided it was time to go. At two o'clock in the morning at the beginning of May, he woke the servant who slept in the room with him.

'Karamanye, belly ache,' he groaned, bending double as if in pain. 'Moola, I'm sick,' he said, adding that he needed to go downstairs into the garden.

As soon as he was outside, Bennelong jumped the fence and was gone.

And so, after all the risk and effort of his capture, all the confidence placed in the scheme and all the rations spared especially for him, Bennelong quickly and quietly took off into the darkness.

Most of the inhabitants of Sydney Cove were too preoccupied with their own hunger and misery to care that the native man, whose arrival had caused so much excitement, had escaped.

Chapter 27

Sydney Cove, June - July 1790

One bleak wintery day Watkin Tench sat in his hut feeling worried and depressed about the future of the colony when an unusual burst of activity outside snapped him out of his gloom. He could hear the sound of women shrieking.

What on earth's going on out there?

The shouting and screaming continued and it quickly registered that they weren't cries of alarm, but calls of excitement. The women seemed to be beside themselves with delight about something! He flung his door open and stood gaping at the scene. Women with dazed looks were running back and forth with children in their arms. They were hugging each other and crying with joy.

'The flag's up...the flag's up!' someone was calling.

Hardly able to contain himself, he grabbed his looking glass and ran to the nearest hill as fast as his legs would carry him. And there he saw it - a tiny sail on the horizon, heralding the arrival of a ship.

Was it a ship from England, carrying supplies and letters from home? Surely it must be! It would be their first news in three years.

A crowd had gathered around him and Watkin Tench felt himself overcome with emotion. Looking out to sea he couldn't stop the tears rolling down his cheeks. He turned to a fellow officer but neither could say a word, they were both too choked.

Stories of Life at Sydney Cove

He describes his emotion in that moment of sheer relief:

> *My next door neighbour, a brother-officer, stood next to me, but we could not speak. We squeezed each other by the hand, with eyes and hearts overflowing.*

Minutes later, Watkin Tench ran back down the hill knowing that the Governor would set out in a boat to meet the ship as it entered the harbour. He prayed silently that this would not be a repeat of their trip when learning of the shipwrecked *Sirius*. On reaching the wharf he was short of breath.

'Please sir, can I join you?' he called. The Governor just nodded and Tench realised that he too was overcome with emotion.

The weather was atrocious that day and rain lashed the faces of the crew, but they rowed with all their strength. Every man was on the same wavelength. They all wanted to know if the ship *really* was from good old England. They all wanted to be out of their misery.

'Pull away, me lads,' the crew urged each other on. 'Nearly there.'

As they neared the entrance to the harbour, they saw a large ship in the distance and soon they made out the word *'London'* on the stern.

'She *is* from Old England!'

'Come on, a few strokes more, and we shall be aboard!'

'Hurrah for a bellyful, and news from our friends!' The boat's crew cheered and yelled into the wind.

News from home at long last!

A few minutes later the men boarded the *'Lady Juliana'* which they soon learnt, carried over two hundred convicts.

****

To everyone's surprise the ship had taken almost eleven months to make the voyage from England to New South Wales; three months longer than the First Fleet. But it had arrived…with food, provisions and letters. The colonists were desperate for news from home and the questions tumbled out, everyone talking at once.

'Letters, letters!' was the cry all around.

When the ship anchored, bundles of mail were distributed and torn open with trembling hands. Some had to find another person to read their letters aloud for them. There was so much news from home it took days to absorb it all.

The Governor learnt that a ship, *HMS Guardian*, had left England the year before with provisions for the colony, but had hit an iceberg in the southern ocean. If that tragedy hadn't occurred, supplies would have reached Sydney Cove in time to prevent the extreme food shortage they'd suffered.

****

Shortly following the arrival of the *Lady Juliana*, another ship entered the harbour loaded entirely with provisions for the colony. At last, the settlers could return to full rations.

By the end of June, a further three ships arrived with convicts, as part of the second fleet of convict ships from England. The state of the prisoners however, showed terrible neglect and cruelty, particularly to those aboard *Neptune*. Many convicts had died on the voyage from starvation and mistreatment. As the ships entered the harbour bodies of the recently dead were thrown overboard before reaching Sydney Cove. The natives were shocked to see putrid, shrunken corpses washed ashore on the secluded beaches away from Sydney.

Once the ships anchored, hundreds of men and women had to be carried ashore and taken to temporary hospital tents where many soon took their last breath. The Governor's secretary, witnessing the horror, wrote:

> *Several of these miserable people died in the boats as they were being rowed onshore, or on the wharf as they were being lifted out of the boats. All this was because of their confinement in a small space and many of them chained together.*
>
> *It was said that on board the Neptune several died in irons, and what added to the horror was that their deaths were concealed, so that their allowance of food could be shared among the living, until by chance, and the smell of a corpse, led the surgeon to the spot where it lay.*

Nanberry and Boorong were among the crowd watching the terrible scene of filthy, limp bodies being brought ashore for John White, as Chief Surgeon of the colony, to try to bring back to health. Nanberry knew his foster father would give the task all the energy he had. He knew John White had done everything in his power to save his own young life, and many other black and white lives, so many times during the past two and a half years.

About five hundred dying or seriously ill convicts were landed from the ships of the second fleet and it tested John White and his assistants to their medical limits. But, despite the lack of hospital beds, blankets and equipment, they managed to save nearly half of them.

****

The second fleet also brought two companies of the newly formed New South Wales Corps. These soldiers were part of a unit put together for service in the colony. Their duties would include guarding the convicts and protecting the colony. They'd been sent to replace the marines who would soon return to England. One member of the newly arrived Corps was Lieutenant John Macarthur with his wife, Elizabeth and their baby son, Edward. Twenty-two year-old Elizabeth had kept a journal during their voyage.

Their journey had quickly developed into an ordeal as they'd had to endure a tiny airless cabin, with only a thin partition dividing them from sick convicts. John Macarthur had also become dangerously ill and little Edward had been so sick that Elizabeth thought she was going to lose him. She wrote of this difficult time:

> *No language can express, no imagination can picture the misery I experienced. In my wretched cabin my spirit failed me and my health deserted me...*

To make matters more distressing, Elizabeth was expecting their second baby. Conditions were so bad that after weeks of anxiety, struggle and lack of sleep, her pregnancy ended. Her baby daughter only lived an hour. The grieving parents had watched helplessly as her tiny body, wrapped in a small canvas blanket, was dropped into the sea.

The day they finally sailed into Sydney Cove was cold, grey and gloomy but they were grateful they'd arrived safely after those awful months of travel. When John Macarthur stepped onto the wooden pier, he was still recovering from his serious illness. Elizabeth was extremely concerned about him and their one-year-old son. However she put on a brave face as she walked the muddy track, across ditches bridged with cut logs, to their two roomed mud and thatched hut on the edge of a dense forest, their new home.

As she made her way between the simple dwellings, dodging puddles as she went, she was aware of the stares of the convicts and the gazes of the officers. She realised that despite her crumpled skirt and mud-stained boots, she was well dressed compared with the faded, tattered and patched clothes of everyone around her.

Elizabeth Macarthur had crossed the oceans of the world, leaving her family and friends behind to be with her husband as he advanced his career in New South Wales. She'd adapted to terrible conditions on the voyage so she wouldn't let the primitive scene of Sydney Cove faze her. It helped to remind herself that their time in the colony was temporary. She believed that when her husband's tour of duty was over, they'd return to England, to her mother, her younger sister and her dear grandfather. During her first months in the settlement however, her focus was on the fragile health of her husband and little son. She was determined to make the best of her situation in their small hut with its earthen floor, leaky roof and glassless windows. With the few belongings she'd brought from England, she began a routine with a show of optimism she didn't feel.

John and Elizabeth soon heard the stories of the colony's near starvation. They listened to accounts of problems with the native people: the injuries, punishments and paybacks. They saw the gallows where the bodies of Englishmen had swung for stealing food. However, they also learnt of the progress being made.

'The colony so far has three settlements; one here at Sydney Cove and one at Rose Hill. And there is also Norfolk Island,' Governor Phillip informed the new arrivals about their expansion.

'How far has the country been explored, Sir?' John Macarthur asked, keen to learn about the colony's prospects.

'About twenty miles out [11]. We'd hoped to find a way across the mountains to the west by now, but it's proved more difficult than first imagined.'

'I see. There's still much to learn then?' the young soldier said.

Governor Phillip sensed ambition in John Macarthur, maybe even overconfidence.

****

A short time after the Macarthurs arrived, an incident occurred in the harbour that made Elizabeth cautious of her new surroundings. A sailor and three marines were in a fishing boat on the harbour when a huge whale raised itself out the water, seemingly intent on hunting them down.

The only survivor, a marine named John Wilkins, retold the gripping story to a rapt audience of officers some days later.

'We'd been out fishing and were heading back when we first saw it. The whale rose out of the water close to us so we rowed with all our might to get away from it. For a while it seemed to disappear and we thought it'd gone. But to our horror, it rose so close to us that the boat filled with water,' the man paused as he relived the fear.

'And, what happened next...?' his friends urged.

'We tried to bale the water out, and at the same time steer away from the monster.' The man hesitated again, remembering.

'For a time we didn't see it, and we thought ourselves safe. Then it suddenly rose right beneath our boat, lifting us a great height from the water. It seemed we were up there on its back a long time and as we slipped off plunging to the water, it felt like...it felt like...'

Everyone waited, seeing his difficulty.

[11] twenty miles = thirty kilometres

'It felt like falling from a cliff top. I don't remember much after that...I hit the water. There was a whirlpool I think and the others got sucked down. I escaped...I just kept swimming to the shore.'

There was silence for a while, everyone feeling the fear.

'Well, you lived to tell the tale, John. You couldn't have done anything for the others. We all know that.'

News of the shocking event spread quickly around the settlement making many of the colonists, including Elizabeth Macarthur, think twice about going on the harbour.

****

There was no doubting the truth of the incident, but Watkin Tench had trouble believing it. Whales were generally docile creatures.

'Had something happened to bring on the attack?' he wondered.

After making enquiries he learnt that sailors from the second fleet had hunted the whale a day earlier with harpoons. It had escaped, but had been injured.

'Mm,' thought Tench, 'A payback?'

****

The first half of 1790 had been dramatic on many levels for everyone at Sydney Cove. The food crisis, the wreck of *HMS Sirius*, and the arrival of the second fleet with sick convicts had all been traumatic. But the next major incident, occurring in September, sent shock waves through the colony.

Chapter 28

Manly Cove, September 1790

The addition of hundreds of convicts, and soldiers of the New South Wales Corps on the second fleet, had meant a busy period for Governor Phillip. But as soon as time allowed, he wanted to continue the important task of connecting with the native people. In particular, he wanted to make contact with Bennelong. He was about to get his wish, but at a cost he could not have imagined.

One day in the first week of September, John White with young Nanberry and several others were on the harbour. As they approached the bay known as Manly Cove, they saw a large group of natives feasting around the whale that had beached itself and died. They were cooking thick slabs of whale meat on several fires when the white men approached by boat.

As this was the first contact between the two groups since Bennelong's escape, both parties were cautious. The natives seeing the boat approach picked up their spears so Nanberry was asked to call out in their language, telling them the white men had friendly intentions.

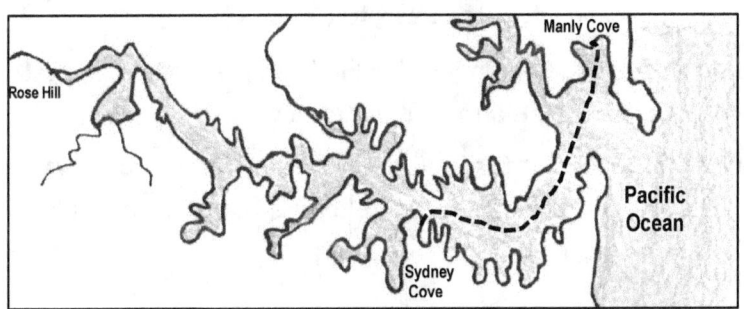

Eventually Bennelong and Colbee came forward and a short conversation followed. They were hesitant at first but seemed willing to forgive their kidnappers. Bennelong asked for some clothes and when he received some, he began to put them on for the amusement of his countrymen who still kept their distance.

As the white men were about to leave, Bennelong expressed a wish to make contact with the Governor and asked the boat crew returning to Sydney to take some whale meat to him. It seemed like a peace offering.

****

As soon as the Governor learnt of the chance to speak with Bennelong, he made immediate plans to go to the meeting place. After collecting food, clothes as gifts, and firearms as back up, he set off by boat to the same beach. David Collins, his secretary and a junior officer, Henry Waterhouse accompanied him. On the way to Manly Cove they tested their muskets but found that only one was working. Governor Phillip had a hand pistol but they had no other weapons. They weren't expecting trouble, so it wasn't a concern.

As Phillip's boat approached the beach, the large group feasting there moved back among the trees. Governor Phillip believed a show of confidence was the best way to re-open communication.

'Stay in the boat,' he said to his officers. 'But have the musket ready just in case.' He told one of the boat crew to follow with bread, meat and a few items as gifts.

'Bennelong!' The Governor called loudly to the group as he walked up the beach with his arms spread to show he was unarmed.

Nobody responded at first and the Governor continued to walk up the beach, toward the trees. Soon he was out of sight of his men waiting in the boat.

Bennelong didn't come forward immediately and when he did, he had changed so much in the five months since his escape that Phillip didn't recognise him. He'd lost weight, had a long beard and more battle scars. He stood at a distance with several other native men.

'Where is Bennelong?' the Governor called as he kept walking toward the group, and further from his boat. A native man approached and Phillip put some items on the sand between them.

'Where is Bennelong?' the Governor asked again.

'I am Bennelong,' the man replied, but Phillip didn't believe it.

He looked nothing like the person he knew as Bennelong. The man in front of him was very thin, bearded and had a lot of recent wounds.

As a way of checking the man's identity, Phillip held up various objects that would be familiar to the real Bennelong.

'Mee diee,' (What's this?) the Governor asked in Bennelong's language pointing to a bottle of wine.

'The King,' the man called, lifting his arm as if holding up a glass.

Phillip knew only Bennelong would say that. He'd sat at his table in Government House with the officers and they had all raised their glasses to drink to His Majesty's health.

The Governor then invited him to accept some gifts. But each time Bennelong went to step closer, he changed his mind and stepped back again. As he continued to back away, the Governor followed him, further and further away from his boat. All the time he tried to convince Bennelong that he wanted to rebuild their friendship.

In the meantime, several groups of natives, with about eight to ten men in each group, placed themselves in locations so that they could prevent Bennelong being grabbed. Once they were in position, Bennelong came forward with Colbee to shake the

Governor's hand. They knew it was the white men's way of greeting.

After a short conversation the Governor returned to the boat to collect more gifts and bring David Collins back with him to meet their old friends.

'Stay here,' he told Henry Waterhouse. 'But keep the boat afloat in case we need to make a quick getaway.' He sensed the natives were edgy and trouble was possible.

Henry Waterhouse could see from his position in the boat that the Governor's movements were being closely watched and relayed between strategically placed natives. The situation seemed tense, but the Governor was clearly happy about the reunion.

Soon the sailor returned to the boat asking Waterhouse to join the Governor on the beach too. Later he recorded what happened:

> *On landing, I observed a number of natives on each side and eight or ten in front all with their spears in their hand, except for the two men speaking with the Governor and Captain Collins. They seemed in deep conversation.*

When Henry Waterhouse reached the group, the atmosphere was relaxed. Bennelong was cheerful and happy to see him, and repeatedly shook the Englishmen's hands. He asked about many of the people he knew at Sydney Cove, mimicking each one's habits.

Colbee was also in a good mood, putting on hats and joking around. He laughingly pointed to his ankle where the leg iron had been attached when he was in Sydney Cove. He demonstrated how he'd removed the metal ring put on his leg by the white men. Then he made a joke about Bennelong's escape.

'Gov'nor nangorar,' (Governor asleep) he said as he mimed sleep by putting his head on his hands with his eyes shut. Still laughing, he imitated how Bennelong had jumped the fence and run off.

At this point another native, who'd been standing back, approached Phillip and showed him several spear wounds on his back. Bennelong also began pointing out injuries that he'd received since leaving the settlement. He had a wound on his arm and another, still looking bad, above his left eye. He explained they'd happened in a conflict at Botany Bay.

As they were speaking, Governor Phillip noticed an unusual spear lying on the ground. It was much longer than any he'd seen before and was tipped with hardwood. Thinking it was particularly interesting, the Governor asked if he could have it but Bennelong placed it on the ground a little distance away.

Up to this point, there'd been friendly conversation and everything seemed to be going well. But when the Governor mentioned the spear, things seemed to change.

The natives appeared to be closing around them in a semicircle. Phillip noticed this and muttered instructions to his men:

'I think we should return to the boat. They're surrounding us.'

The mood had definitely altered. About twenty armed men had formed a crescent around them and the Englishmen knew there were many more that they couldn't see. Phillip addressed Bennelong in a calm manner.

'We will go now but I will return in two days. I will bring more clothes, like those you wore in Sydney Cove, and some hatchets,' he said as evenly as he could, as they started edging away.

But Bennelong began delaying them. He introduced them to some natives who were nearby. Then he pointed to a stranger standing near the unusual spear, as if he wanted the Governor to notice this particular man. The Governor walked toward him, putting out his hand as a greeting. And that's when it happened...

As the native stepped back with one foot and took aim, Phillip instantly saw danger and called out in the man's language.

 'Weeree, Weeree,' (Bad! You are doing wrong)

The words were barely out of his mouth, when the spear hit him with incredible force just above the collarbone. It penetrated so deeply that the point stuck out through his back, between his spine and shoulder blade. When the attacker saw his weapon had struck, he dashed into the forest.

There was instant confusion. Bennelong and Colbee disappeared while several spears flew through the air, though none hit the Englishmen. Henry Waterhouse was in complete panic and wrote about it later.

At first I thought the governor was killed, as the spear appeared to me much lower than it really was, and I supposed there was no chance for any of us to escape. But I turned to run for the beach as I saw Collins running that way and calling to the boat crew to bring the muskets.

The governor also attempted to run holding the spear with both hands to keep the end of it off the ground...

The Governor was in intense pain. The spear was almost three metres long, and sticking out in front of him. As he tried to run down the beach to the boat, the end of the shaft kept striking the ground, tearing the gash of his wound even further open.

'For God's sake, haul the spear out!' he pleaded, as the other men began heading down the beach toward the boat.

Waterhouse immediately turned and began tugging at the spear, but saw that by pulling the barb back through the Governor's chest he was causing more damage. Instead, he tried in vain to break off the shaft without adding to the Governor's agony. He describes how a surge of fear helped accomplish the task:

> *Just in that instant, another spear came and grazed the skin between the thumb and finger of my right hand. I must admit it frightened me a good deal and I believe added to my effort because with the next sudden jerk, it broke off.*

As the men struggled down the beach toward the boat, one of the crew appeared and fired a shot toward the trees with the only working musket. Eventually they made it to the boat with the Governor leaning heavily against Waterhouse. When the men lifted him into the boat, he was very faint. He was also losing a lot of blood.

On the way back to Sydney Cove, they couldn't stop the Governor's bleeding and they all thought he was going to die. When they arrived at Sydney Cove, a sailor raced to fetch a doctor urgently.

'How many hours do I have to live?' Phillip gasped as the doctor examined him.

When the spearhead was carefully removed, the doctor assured the Governor he would recover.

'You must rest for at least six weeks, and if you do, you will be able to go about your business again as usual,' the doctor told him.

As he was healing Phillip had plenty of time to think over the event.

Why had it happened? What had triggered the attack?

Maybe the natives thought Bennelong would be kidnapped again?

Over and over, he went through each step of the incident. He thought about the man who had speared him.

'I would like to meet that man,' he told Lieutenant Waterhouse, 'not to punish him, but to ask him why... I want to know why.'

He considered the timing of the attack. It was at the end of the visit, in full view of the natives surrounding him.

If it had been the warrior's plan to throw the spear all along, why didn't he do it when I was alone on the beach?
Why did he wait till Waterhouse and Collins were there?

Phillip wanted to believe it was an accident, but things puzzled him. He was still trying to make sense of it all when he wrote about the event in his journal:

> *It is most likely that the action came from a fleeting impulse of fear. But the behaviour of Bennelong on this occasion is not so easily explained. He never attempted to interfere when the man took the spear up, or said a single word to prevent him throwing it.*

Why hadn't Bennelong tried to stop it?
Why hadn't **he** *called out, 'Weeree, Weeree'?*

Then Phillip reflected on the placement of the native men on the beach. Their positions showed planning. He thought about the weapon. The spear had a smooth wooden head. From what he knew, it wasn't a weapon of execution. Its plunge wasn't meant to be fatal.

The Governor then thought about the way the natives had shown him their wounds just before the attack.

Why had they done that?
Had they shown him their wounds to demonstrate that it was their
way of dealing with serious abuse of law?
Was it an example of their payback punishment?

In the end the Governor didn't know what to think, but officially he
declared it had *not* been deliberate violence.

'We will put the attack down to fear; the man who speared me
thought I meant to harm him. It happened in the heat of the
moment, it wasn't planned,' he told everyone who asked.

'Do you think we should take some action, Sir?' his officers asked.
'Is it wise to ignore the incident, whether or not it was intended?'

'I want strict orders given that none of the natives are to be fired
on. We must look to the future. I don't want this affair to hinder a
peaceful outcome with the natives,' Phillip said decisively.

'Yes Sir,' the officers replied. They could see their Governor had a
firm view on the issue.

'It is my intention, as soon as I am able, to try to find Bennelong
again. I need to get to the bottom of this affair.'

They would all get over this.
He would make sure they did.

Chapter 29

Sydney Cove, September - November 1790

In the days following the attack on the Governor, two native men in a canoe approached officers on the harbour. Using signs they asked about the Governor's condition and showed they were pleased he'd recover. One of the native men said his name was Maugoran. He told them his daughter was Boorong, and that he knew she was alive because the white people had saved her.

Later, Maugoran approached a boat and asked the white men to give their leader a message. This time Boorong was with Reverend Johnson and she acted as go-between. Her father asked Boorong to tell the white men he was from the area the British called 'Rose Hill'.

She explained that her father was a *Burramattagal* (one of the people of Burramatta). His people had lived at the head of the harbour long before white settlers moved there. Many native families had since had to relocate to other places along the river.

'Burramattagal are not happy that many white people live at Rose Hill,' Boorong told the Reverend. 'They want the Gov'nor to know.'

The Governor got the message and thought over the issue before discussing it with his officers. One thing was plain to him. The native people still didn't understand his good intentions toward them.

Wasn't it clear to them that he wanted a peaceful relationship? Hadn't he tried to involve them?

'If the information passed on by the man named Maugoran is true, they're very angry that so many settlers are at Rose Hill,' Phillip said to his gathered officers.

'I just wish we could persuade some to settle *in* Rose Hill,' he added sounding tired and frustrated. It was only a week since his attack. 'My aim has always been to furnish them with everything that can civilise them. I want them to have a high opinion of us.'

'If only we could communicate better, Sir,' said Lieutenant Dawes. 'I'm adding words to the language list I began with Arabanoo, and continue with Boorong and Nanberry. But we need much more.'

'What you're doing will certainly help, Dawes. Good work.'

'In the meantime Sir, what do you suggest in light of this information from the native man?' an officer stationed at Rose Hill asked.

'Well, if there *is* trouble at Rose Hill, the number of soldiers already there won't be able to stop it. We'll have to add to the military presence as soon as possible.'

'I will see to it then Sir.'

****

As Maugoran paddled back to his family along the river, he wondered if his appeal to the white leader would be heard. He had mixed and conflicting thoughts about the people living at Warran (Sydney Cove). They had saved his daughter's life. On the other hand, they had taken his land.

The next day Maugoran watched as more soldiers arrived at Rose Hill. He didn't know what to think.

Stories of Life at Sydney Cove

Several days later the two native children, Nanberry and Boorong were on the harbour with John White and Reverend Johnson. They saw a fire on the beach at Manly Cove and took it as a signal for them to visit. On landing, they met a group of men, including Bennelong.

The British men offered food and other gifts they had in their boat. Bennelong was in high spirits and took the leading role, sharing the bread and beef with his native friends. He asked the white men to shave him and his friends laughed as they watched the process. They wouldn't agree to be shaved themselves, but were pleased to have their beards trimmed with scissors.

A native woman stood at a distance observing the get-together with interest. The white men signaled for her to join their group but she was hesitant.

'Barangaroo,' Bennelong boasted seeing the white men notice her, 'She's my wife now.'

They remembered he had spoken a lot about this special woman when he was in Sydney Cove. They knew she must have a great influence on Bennelong and wanted to meet her too. The Reverend asked Boorong to take a petticoat to Barangaroo, and to coax her to join them.

'Mee diee,' (What's this?) Barangaroo asked as the girl came near.

'A petticoat,' said Boorong explaining that she should put it over her head and put her arms through the other holes.

'Wen,' (Let's walk) Barangaroo suggested simply in their language.

The men watched as the two young women strolled away together along the beach, already deep in conversation. Barangaroo had many questions she wanted to ask about the strangers who had so strongly caught Bennelong's attention.

Boorong tried to answer her questions, but she had difficulty explaining some of the aspects of life at Sydney Cove. One thing she stressed to Barangaroo was that clothes were very important to the white people.

When they returned from their walk, Barangaroo joined the group wearing the petticoat. However, she wasn't as eager as Bennelong to try the white men's other offerings. She had a little sip of the drink they called 'wine' but spat it out.

'Weeree!' (No good) she declared, adding she'd never try it again.

She also made it very clear to the white men, speaking through Bennelong and Boorong, she didn't intend visiting the British campsite. The white people had strange ways. They'd snatched her Bennelong, they'd brought injury and disease to her people and even recently, they'd stolen their precious hunting and fishing equipment. The white men promised they would look into the thefts and return the following day to replace the stolen property.

When the time came to get back in the boat to return to Sydney Cove, Boorong became very quiet.

'I want to stay here,' she told the Reverend. 'Like it here.'

'Come now Boorong. We will come back again tomorrow. Ma'am and little Milbah will miss you if you don't come home today.'

After some coaxing, Boorong eventually got into the boat but sat sulking all the way across the harbour to Sydney Cove. She was thinking over all the things she had discussed with Barangaroo. She was remembering life with her people and all the things she missed.

The British men returned to Sydney Cove not doubting Barangaroo's claim of theft and made a search of the settlement for stolen goods. The following day, they returned across the harbour as promised with a large quantity of recovered property. Watkin Tench gave the details of its return to its owners:

> *When all the stolen property was brought on shore, an old man came up and claimed one of the fishing spears, singling it from the bundle, taking only his own. This honesty, within the circle of their society, seemed to characterize them all...*
>
> *Among other things, was a net full of fishing lines and other tackle, which Barangaroo said was her property and, immediately on receiving it, she slung it around her neck.*

The white men asked Bennelong to visit the Governor who was still recovering from his injury, but he hesitated.

'You can leave again anytime you want,' the men promised.

Bennelong shook his head, insisting that the Governor must visit him first.

As soon as he heard this, Phillip got out of his bed and gingerly climbed into a boat and was rowed across the harbour to meet with Bennelong. It was only ten days after the removal of the spear but he was keen to make contact. When they met, he assured Bennelong again that if he came to Sydney in future, he would have complete freedom.

'You will come and go as you please, Bennelong,' Phillip promised him.

****

A few weeks later, Bennelong decided it was time to visit the Governor at Sydney Cove but it didn't happen without serious trouble between him and Barangaroo. Earlier the same day, there'd been a friendly gathering between a group of white people and natives at Manly Cove. Among the group was Reverend Johnson, Watkin Tench, Boorong, Bennelong, Barangaroo and others.

The native men had asked to be shaved. The groups exchanged items, and everyone was happily involved in the meeting. When some of the white men left to return to Sydney Cove, Bennelong announced he'd follow them and visit the Governor.

On hearing this, Barangaroo put on a tantrum, crying and objecting loudly, and stamping the ground. When she saw that tears and shouting wouldn't change Bennelong's mind she became very angry, snatched up his fishing spears and threw them against the rocks. She used such force that they broke into pieces. The atmosphere became tense.

Reverend Johnson could see that Barangaroo was very worried that Bennelong wouldn't return from Sydney Cove. As a guarantee of his safe return, he offered to remain at Manly Cove as a hostage.

'I will stay here with you, till Bennelong comes back,' he promised.

Barangaroo could see that Bennelong had made up his mind to go. She nodded sulkily but was clearly not happy about it. Bennelong and a group of his friends immediately launched their canoes and paddled across the harbour to visit Governor Phillip.

****

On hearing of Bennelong's arrival, a crowd gathered at the wharf to greet him.

'Hello Bennelong!' people shouted from all directions.

Pleased with the welcome but eager to visit the Governor, he continued along the path to Government House. His curious native friends followed him.

Bennelong and Phillip greeted each other warmly, and bread and meat was served to the visitors.

After that, Bennelong decided to give his friends a tour of the Governor's house, leading them around and pointing to things and naming them. Watkin Tench described the scene in his journal:

> *Bennelong seemed to consider himself quite at home, running from room to room with his companions, and introducing them to his old friends, the servants in the most familiar manner. Some of these he kissed with great affection, in particular a woman who worked in the kitchen.*

He showed his friends all the things in the Governor's house new to them, explaining the use of different furniture, demonstrating how things worked like candles, cooking pots, hinges and keys.

Outside he showed them a wheelbarrow, a ladder and blacksmith's tools. Bennelong clearly enjoyed airing his knowledge to his friends and he was in his element being the centre of attention.

Seeing children near the Governor's garden, he greeted them warmly, remembering each one's name.

'Hello young Harry,' he called brightly, when Susannah brought her son to greet Bennelong.

'Hello Bennelong,' the boy replied, smiling up at the kind man who had always made time for him. All the children loved Bennelong. He was good at mimicking the way different people at Sydney Cove walked and talked. It made the children laugh to watch him.

Back at the wharf, people gathered around to greet Bennelong again and he was pleased to see them. The only person in the whole settlement that Bennelong and the other native men deliberately avoided was a convict named John McEntire. Tench noticed this, and wrote in his journal that they showed 'dread and hatred' for that particular man.

As soon as the men finished their tour, Watkin Tench and others went back across the harbour with Bennelong's party to collect Reverend Johnson and Boorong. As they approached the beach, they saw Barangaroo sitting beside a fire making fishhooks, and the Reverend sitting near her. Boorong was in a canoe fishing close to the shore. It was a peaceful scene ending a momentous day. Bennelong's visit to the settlement with his friends signaled a new phase for life at Sydney Cove.

****

Following Bennelong's visit to the Governor, friendly contact continued between them. Even Barangaroo's distrust of the British softened and she willingly came to Sydney Cove with her husband.

Soon others came to stay in the settlement for days at a time. As the number of Aboriginal families increased in Sydney Cove, language barriers were overcome with signs, gestures and good humour on both sides. Bennelong was the man everyone went to with questions about customs and language problems.

Elizabeth Macarthur, who'd arrived in the colony just after Bennelong's escape, was keen to meet the man who everyone described as funny, intelligent and intriguing. In a letter to her friend in England, she described the change that his visit brought to Sydney Cove from October 1790:

> *Since that period the natives visit us every day, more or less. Men, women and children come with great confidence without spears or any weapon. A great many live among us and Bennelong and Colbee with their wives come in frequently.*
>
> *Mrs Colbee, whose name is Daringa, brought in a newborn female infant of hers for me to see...The baby was wrapped up in the soft bark of a tree.*

At Bennelong's request, the Governor had a brick house built for him at a place he chose along the headland from Government House. This place became a meeting spot for his people, and was known as Bennelong's Point[12].

William Dawes, the young officer living at the observatory on Sydney Cove's western point, was delighted to have visits from Bennelong's friends. They knew he was interested in their culture and keen to add more of their words and phrases to his notebook. They stayed for hours patiently repeating expressions for him, as he wrote them down. Boorong and Nanberry were among the group that sat in the sunshine on the warm, flat rock shelf in front of his hut.

[12] Bennelong Point is the site of the Sydney Opera House.

Dawes learnt that they referred to themselves as 'Eora', meaning 'the people'. The place where he lived, they called 'Tara'.

Between his hours of duty, Watkin Tench also enjoyed spending time there with Dawes and their new native friends. There was joking and loud laughter if anyone made a mistake saying a new word. Boorong and her friends chuckled at the men's efforts to pronounce certain sounds.

'How do you say *laughter*,' Dawes asked, enjoying the carefree moment. He waited with his pencil ready.

'Dyennibbe,' someone said quickly. When Dawes tried saying the word, they all laughed till tears flowed down their cheeks. The way he'd said it was clearly not correct.

'The sound *dy* is difficult for English mouths,' Tench said, also enjoying the relaxed atmosphere. 'But we'll keep trying.'

Dawes added the word for 'laughter' to his notebook, writing it in a simple way he could remember:

> *Dyennibbe* = *laughter (Jen-ne-be)*
> *Eora* = *people*

The white men knew the Eora were very good at remembering English words, but they had problems with some sounds too. Watkin Tench wrote in his journal:

> *The 's' is a letter they cannot pronounce, having no sound in their language similar to it. When trying to pronounce 'sun', they always say 'tun'. When saying 'salt', they say 'talt', and so on...*

****

Another young woman named Patyegarang became a regular visitor at Dawes' gatherings and the two became close friends. The group spent lighthearted hours sharing stories, songs and customs. They were comfortable in each other's company, making mistakes, laughing and learning from each other.

'I think I'll apply to stay on in Sydney Cove, when the time comes to decide, Tench.' William Dawes confided in his friend. 'Now that things are more settled, I feel there's so much I can learn here.'

'I'm not surprised you feel that way Dawes, and I understand. But I'll be happy to get home to England,' Tench admitted.

'Barangaroo and Bennelong were at my house yesterday with a big group of others,' Dawes smiled remembering the incident. 'Bennelong asked me to shave him, and while I had the razor in my hand, Boorong joked to Barangaroo that I might cut her husband with it. Everyone laughed, knowing it was meant to be funny. I think that shows how far we've come, don't you?'

'Yes Dawes,' Watkin Tench said as they strolled along the track from the observatory. 'Like you, I feel affection for these people and I know we can learn a lot from them.'

****

While cultural relations were progressing well around Sydney Cove, James Ruse the convict farmer, and his wife Elizabeth, were working hard at Rose Hill. They'd cleared large areas of land and planted vegetables and crops of wheat and corn. He was experimenting with different times for planting because the seasons were different to England. He'd made compost with rotting leaves, dry grass, manure and ashes from their fire. Ruse knew he had to add this fertilizer to the soil to improve his crops. He'd been on 'Experiment Farm' nearly one year, and though he knew there was much more to do, he was making headway.

****

Bennelong and Colbee with their wives, extended families and many friends continued to visit and stay in Sydney Cove. The Governor, who Bennelong still called Be-anna (father), had offered the Eora unrestricted access to the settlement. He had promised them an ongoing supply of provisions: bread, meat, rice, iron hatchets, blankets and clothes. They could come and go as they pleased the Governor had told them.

The brick house, built for Bennelong on the eastern point of Sydney Cove became his 'headquarters'. It was where his people met to talk, plan, sing and dance.

'It seems the attack on the Governor is now forgotten.' Tench said one day to William Dawes, as they watched Barangaroo and her husband arrive at the Governor's house for dinner.

Bennelong and his companions were happy with their decision to stay with the British people at Sydney Cove. But not all the Eora agreed with their choice.

Chapter 30

Botany Bay - Sydney Cove, December 1790

One of the people who didn't share Bennelong's confidence in the white people was a native man called Pemulwuy. He was a tall, muscular warrior whose name meant 'man of the earth'. He believed the people of Sydney Cove were responsible for bad things happening to his people, and he thought the time had come for him to do something about it.

Pemulwuy

****

The year 1790 had been challenging for everyone at Sydney Cove, but especially for Governor Phillip. He'd faced difficult decisions over food shortages. He'd had the shocking news of the wreck of the government ship *Sirius*. The arrival of the second fleet brought sick convicts and many more mouths to feed. And last but not least, the spearing attack that had left him with a scar he would always carry. If the white leader was hoping that the year would end without further drama, he was in for disappointment.

****

Phillip was away at Rose Hill when a disturbing event occurred in bushland south of Sydney. The drama centred on a convict named John McEntire, a skilled hunter who supplied meat for the Governor's household. At the same time, this man was strongly disliked by the Aboriginal people around Sydney Cove, including Pemulwuy.

At the beginning of December, McEntire and two other convicts under the supervision of a soldier, set out on an overnight hunting trip to the Botany Bay area. Their plan was to rest till late afternoon, then hunt kangaroos while they grazed in the early evening. The group had settled down for an afternoon nap in a bark hut, when they heard rustling sounds outside in the bushes. One of the men peered out between the cracks and spotted a number of natives creeping toward the hut.

'Don't be afraid, I know them,' McEntire told his wide-eyed, frightened companions.

He advised the other men to stay put, assuring them he would fix things. He left the shelter unarmed and walked toward the natives, speaking to them in their language. One of the eyewitnesses later reported that at first the natives appeared to back away from McEntire, then one of them without warning, launched his spear at him, embedding it in his left side. From the view inside the hut, the violent attack seemed to be unnecessary. McEntire doubled over, immediately sensing he was in serious trouble.

'I'm a dead man,' he cried. 'Get me back home. I don't want to die out here.'

His companions broke the wooden shaft, leaving the spearhead embedded, and immediately began a slow trip back to Sydney Cove carrying the patient. McEntire was losing a lot of blood, and it wasn't till early morning that they staggered into the settlement.

When the doctor examined his wound, he knew it was too late to save him. McEntire knew it too. The spearhead, still stuck in his side, was no ordinary hunting weapon. He'd seen this type of spear before and knew how it worked. If an attempt was made to extract it, the small stone barbs attached along the tip, would tear off and lodge inside him. He was a goner!

'Oh God have mercy on me,' the dying man wailed, mumbling to himself about the dreadful things he had done.

The following day, Colbee was questioned about the man who'd thrown the spear at McEntire. He said the attacker's name was Pemulwuy, 'a man of distinction' from the Botany Bay district. Colbee also confirmed the surgeon's suspicion. If the doctor tried to extract the spearhead, death would be immediate. If it was left in the man's side, he would linger, but he would not recover.

McEntire lived for a few weeks, but before his death, he denied any guilt about his treatment of native people. Watkin Tench and William Dawes discussed the issue. It seemed the Governor believed the wounded man was innocent, while others doubted it.

'Soon after the attack, McEntire muttered confessions about his dealings with the natives,' Tench said to Dawes. 'But later when the Governor questioned him, his story was different. He said he'd only ever shot at natives in self-defence.'

'Well, judging by the natives' reaction to McEntire whenever they saw him, there's more to it than that,' said Dawes. 'From what I've heard, I can't believe he's innocent.'

'Well the Governor questioned all three men with McEntire when he was speared, and they all said McEntire did nothing that day to deserve the attack.'

'Maybe not that day... Anyway, the Governor is convinced the man called Pemulwuy attacked McEntire for no good reason. And he's extremely troubled by the whole affair,' Tench commented.

The McEntire incident was the last straw in what had been a difficult year for Phillip. His reaction to the attack was unexpected and dramatic. He felt it needed a strong response, and had it announced:

> *The Governor, in order to deter the natives from such practices in future, has ordered out a party to search for the man who wounded the convict McEntire in so dangerous a manner on Friday last, though no offence was offered on his part...*

Events were about to take a turn for the worse.

****

Governor Phillip paced the room waiting for Watkin Tench to attend a private meeting in his office. When the officer arrived the Governor informed him he was to lead an expedition to find and punish the attacker Pemulwuy, and those with him. Tench stood to attention as Phillip gave his orders.

'You are to proceed to Botany Bay and if practicable, bring away two natives as prisoners, and to put to death ten,' he said firmly. 'You are not to destroy any huts, or harm any women or children.'

Watkin Tench stood before the Governor trying to keep his expression blank, but his heart was pounding. Had he heard correctly? The words, 'put to death ten...' echoed in his head.

He wanted to question such severe action, but it wasn't his place. Phillip however sensed his unspoken question.

'My reason for taking such action is that since arriving in Sydney Cove, quite a number of our people have been killed or injured by the natives. I believe the main attackers are from the Botany Bay tribe, and I'm determined to send a message that will hopefully prevent further deaths.'

'But why such extreme action?' Watkin wanted to ask. Instead he stood silently, knowing he must not interrupt.

'I've delayed the use of violence for so long,' Phillip said, 'as I believed in past attacks, the natives acted because of harm done to them. I think other cases, such as my own injury, happened because of misunderstanding. But this business with McEntire... I'm convinced it was unprovoked. I interviewed the witnesses, the soldier and the two convicts, separately. Each man's story was short, simple, and alike...' The Governor shrugged.

'I've tried in vain to involve Bennelong, Colbee and others to bring in the attacker. Yesterday they promised to do it and went off as if to deal with it. Then I hear they'd gone off on some other activity. So we have only our efforts to depend on...'

The Governor looked directly at Watkin Tench before continuing.

'I plan to execute the prisoners you bring in. The punishment for this crime must be done publically in the presence of as many of their people as can be gathered, after explaining the cause of the punishment to them.'

Here the Governor paused and sighed heavily. His sincere hope had been to keep peace with the natives. He'd always firmly declared that none of their blood would be deliberately shed...but a response to the death of an unarmed man now seemed absolutely necessary.

He was at his wit's end. The responsibility he carried on his shoulders was immense. He looked at his loyal officer, and said purposefully:

'If you can suggest any alternative, I am prepared to listen to you.'

Encouraged by the chance of lessening the impact of his mission, Tench put forward a softer approach:

'Sir, instead of executing ten, would not the capture of six serve the same purpose, and out of that number, execute only some of the captives? The rest, after witnessing the executions, could be released?'

The Governor agreed immediately to adopt his officer's suggestion. As Watkin Tench left the room, Phillip felt the weight of his decision.

Had he been hasty?

It was a terrible situation. There would be no winners.

****

Watkin Tench walked away from the Governor's headquarters feeling very downhearted. Only days before he had thought how harmonious life had become...and now this.

He went to see his friend William Dawes at the observatory. He was not looking forward to his reaction when he learnt he must go on the expedition. They had both developed close friendships among the Eora, but Tench knew that Dawes' connection with some of them was particularly strong. A deep bond of mutual respect had grown between Dawes and his native friends, and Tench expected a strong reaction from him. In this, he was not wrong.

'No!' declared William Dawes. 'I will not do it...I will not go!'

Tench tried to reason with his distressed friend, but Dawes had made up his mind.

'Tench, I cannot, and will not, take part in such an expedition.'

With shaking hands Dawes began writing a letter of refusal to his senior officer. Tench could see his friend was distraught but felt he had to point out the seriousness of his decision.

'Dawes, you do realise you can be arrested for disobeying such an order, don't you?' Tench blurted, but it had no effect.

When his senior officer received the letter, he also pointed out the consequences to Dawes. He would face court-martial[13]. But Dawes would not change his mind. That is, until finally very late that evening the Reverend Johnson was woken and asked to speak to Dawes. After a long and intense discussion, the young man agreed to obey Governor Phillip's instructions. He was reminded of his duty. He must follow orders, without question.

****

The expedition set off at four o'clock the following morning to Botany Bay. The group included several officers, two surgeons and forty soldiers, besides Lieutenants Tench and Dawes, all together about fifty men.

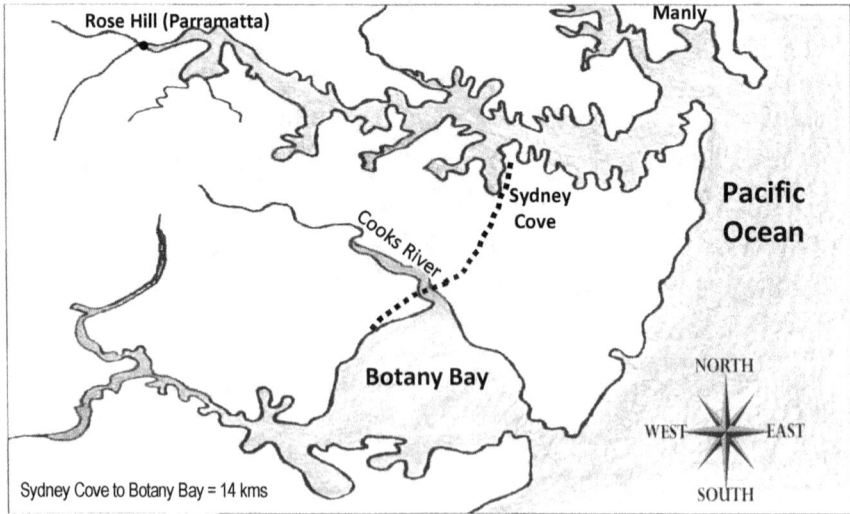

---

[13] court-martial = a military court to decide guilt and punishment

It was mid-December, close to the hottest part of the year. The soldiers wore tight-fitting, long-sleeved, red woollen jackets and black trousers and carried backpacks with provisions for three days. They reached Botany Bay during the morning and began their search for captives. By four in the afternoon, after twelve hours marching and searching they hadn't seen one single native. They set up camp, planning to begin their search again early next morning.

At daylight, they set out again but found themselves at dead ends created by gorges and swamps, and wasted hours retracing their steps. By noon of the second day, they still hadn't met anyone.

As they began their return journey to Sydney, they saw a lone fisherman out in the shallow bay. Although they were on a mission to shoot natives or seize hostages, Tench wasn't keen to do either. He made a note in his journal about the incident:

> *I decided to pass without noticing him, as he seemed quite unafraid at seeing us. Then he called to several of us by name, and came nearer with great confidence.*

To Tench's surprise, the fisherman was their friend Colbee. He said Nanberry told him about the expedition, and when he'd visited the Governor to say he was heading to Botany Bay, the Governor had tried to talk him out of it. Colbee told Tench that Pemulwuy was so far away they wouldn't catch up with him without fresh supplies. After giving that information, Colbee walked with Tench's group, sat and ate lunch with them, had a midday nap and then said goodbye.

It had been a stressful, exhausting day for the British men lugging heavy packs in the summer heat. They were dusty, edgy and very sweaty.

That evening the group camped near a freshwater swamp but the following morning the men struggled out of their blankets complaining of a sleepless night due to the mosquitoes and sand flies that bit and stung them.

They headed homeward tired and grumpy. At low tide they waded chest-deep through stretches of water too wide to go around, arriving back in Sydney by mid-afternoon. Tench reported to the Governor that their expedition had been unsuccessful.

****

To Tench's dismay, the Governor decided they must head out again a week later. As it was a full moon, this time the expedition set off at night.

Leaving Sydney Cove after sunset, they headed south to Botany Bay by the light of the moon. As a short-cut they waded across stretches of water carrying their firearms and ammunition on their heads, carefully dodging large rocks and holes.

Eventually they came to a wide creek. The tide was low so it looked shallow enough to walk through. Tench decided it would save valuable time if they crossed the water instead of marching the long way around the area. However, the first men into the water hadn't reached half way, when it became clear something was very wrong.

'Help! I'm sinking, 'I can't move!' was echoed on every side from soldiers suddenly realising their danger.

It was a distressing situation, particularly as it was happening in the darkness. Every moment became more urgent as the men felt themselves sucked deeper into the thick, gluggy mud. Watkin Tench was already some way into the water when the warning came, and it was too late to turn back.

He later wrote an account of what happened:

> *We became stuck nearly to the waist in mud so thick it was only with the most vigorous effort of every muscle of the body, that we could free ourselves. When we reached the middle, our distress became serious, and each step buried us deeper. Soon one soldier was completely stuck and declared it was impossible to move either forward or backward. Just after, I felt myself in a similar difficulty.*

Fortunately, not all the men had stepped off the bank when the cries of their companions warned them of the danger. A soldier, quickly assessing the situation, cut branches from trees and used them as lifelines for the stranded soldiers. It was a near disaster. One of the men was buried to his armpits and it took the effort of many men to drag him out with the aid of ropes.

It had been a lucky escape but they were all soaking wet, shaken and covered in thick mud that oozed from their boots and weighed them down. But they had no time to rest. It was almost morning so they had to push forward, obey orders and complete their task. They headed to an area where they knew there was a native campsite, but when they got there, they saw it had been deserted for days. By now the men were almost dropping with fatigue. They had marched all night, waded through several rivers and nearly drowned, only to have a failed ambush.

They were aching and frustrated, and still covered in dried mud. All they wanted to do was rest, but that wasn't possible. They had to keep marching to reach a stretch of water before high tide cut them off. Some men said they couldn't keep going.

Tench knew if they didn't continue marching, they'd be trapped on the southern side of the waterway for hours. Their provisions had been left on the other side. He recorded his instructions for dealing with the problem:

> *Our effort was so extreme and our progress so difficult that several of the soldiers gave up, and said they couldn't go any further.*
>
> *All that I could do for these poor fellows was to order their comrades to carry their muskets, and to leave them with a small party of men who were least exhausted, to assist them.*

They all eventually reached and crossed the water in time. They rested during the hottest part of the day, before continuing their march homeward. That day they didn't see a single native person.

They returned to Sydney, to report another unsuccessful expedition.

****

Lieutenant Dawes had struggled with his conscience throughout the excursion. He made a bold statement on his return to Sydney.

'I'm sorry I was talked into following the order, and I'll tell the Governor so,' he told Tench. 'I'll also tell him that in future, I will definitely not obey a similar command.'

The Governor, hearing Dawes' declaration, could not allow such a show of rebellion. He demanded an apology, but the young officer was not prepared to give in.

Under normal circumstances, Dawes would have been arrested, but in Sydney Cove their situation was unusual. Dawes' experience and skills were required in their remote location. Governor Phillip decided to let it go, but made a report against the young officer. He knew Dawes planned to stay in the colony for a further three years, and he would make it difficult for him.

****

Later, when it was all over, Phillip discussed Tench's Botany Bay mission with his secretary, David Collins.

'I know there was little chance of such a large expedition of men surprising and catching the people they were sent to punish.'

'That's true, Sir,' Collins agreed.

'But the very threat of a party being armed and sent purposely to punish Pemulwuy and the group who attacked McEntire, was likely to have the effect we wanted.'

'Let's hope so, Sir,' replied Collins.

****

In the meantime, the Eora community was deciding how to respond to the white leader's military operation. Bennelong and others could see the advantages in their relationship with the British settlers. They would continue trying to understand the ways of the people at Sydney Cove.

Pemulwuy had a different viewpoint. He had avoided the white men by fading back into the wilderness, but he was not finished with the British yet...

He would wait for the right time, but he would never back down.

Chapter 31

Sydney Cove, January - March 1791

The first day of 1791 was declared a public holiday and the people of Sydney Cove began the year on a positive note. With many Eora families now living in Sydney Cove, the place had a colourful and culturally diverse atmosphere.

However, it was the settlers' hottest summer yet. Streams around the cove began to dry up and fresh water became limited. Elizabeth Macarthur, experiencing her first summer in the colony, realised she had never before appreciated the importance of rain.

She began to welcome the rumble of distant thunder in the hope of a pounding downpour. Like other households, the Macarthurs then caught water in buckets, bowls and whatever else they could find. Except for brief storms, there was very little rain.

In late summer, the weather became so hot that settlers saw bats and birds drop out of the trees. Watkin Tench wrote in his journal:

> *An immense flight of bats driven by the wind, covered all the trees around the settlement, but unable to endure the burning atmosphere, they dropped to the ground, dead or dying.*

One day at Rose Hill, Tench recorded the temperature at 2 o'clock in the afternoon to be 109° F.

---

* 109° degrees Fahrenheit = almost 43° degrees Celsius

'It feels like the blast of an oven out there,' Tench said to John and Elizabeth Macarthur when he called to visit them. 'The hot wind is scorching everything in the gardens. It's unbelievable!'

'I can't go out in this heat. I shut myself inside and close everything up to keep the hot air out.' Elizabeth said fanning herself. 'Have you seen the poor birds lying dead on the ground? I left water out for them, but it dried up in minutes.'

****

Despite the heat and the drought, James Ruse saw progress on his farm. In March 1791 he made an announcement to Governor Phillip.

'Your Excellency,' he began, 'I'm happy to say that I've just got in me crop of corn. And I believe I can support me self 'n me wife from the produce of our plot o' land from now on.'

'Well done Ruse. I've followed your progress with great interest. You're a hard worker and deserve everything you've worked for. I intend to grant the allotment of ground at Rose Hill to you. Are you sure you're ready to be totally independent of government support?'

'Yes, Your Excellency, quite sure,' Ruse replied, standing tall.

It was one of the proudest days of his life. He returned to Rose Hill to share the news with his wife. He was a free man, and soon to be owner of his farm.

'I never dreamt it possible, to have me own place,' he said.

****

James Ruse's announcement was the best news Governor Phillip had received for a long time. He sat enjoying the satisfaction it brought him. Ruse had achieved his amazing result after only fifteen months working his plot. He'd proved the doubters wrong. He had shown this country held promise.

****

The eastern headland at Sydney Cove, known as Bennelong's Point, continued to be a hub of activity for the Eora. They met daily to talk around their fire and celebrate life with song, dance and music.

One evening in March, Governor Phillip and his officers were invited to attend a special performance and told to arrive after sunset. As they walked to Bennelong's place, they saw several fires lit and a crowd assembled. The performers' bodies were decorated with streaks of white clay. With the dancers ready, Bennelong and Colbee directed the audience to form a semicircle for a good view.

The evening was so enjoyable for Captain John Hunter, he recorded the details in his journal, describing the dances in particular:

> *One of the most striking moves was made by placing their feet very wide apart, and by an extraordinary action of the muscles of the legs, they moved their knees in a trembling manner.*

Some of the white men had tried to copy the movement, to the entertainment and laughter of everyone.

John Hunter gave more details about the music and dancing at the event. It was the first time he had seen anything like it:

> There was a good deal of variety in their different dances. In one they paired themselves and danced back to back, then they changed suddenly and faced each other.
>
> Sometimes all the performers sat on the ground, and at a particular word they all jumped up, without any assistance from their hands. Then they formed a circle with a person in the centre, and all the performers held a green bough in their hands.
>
> In all the different moves they performed, I observed that they finished with a number of dancers at the front and went through that favourite part of the dance, the quivering motion of the knees. Whenever this was done, the whole company faced the front.
>
> Their music consisted of two sticks of very hard wood, one of which the musician held and struck with the other in regular time. The performer, who was a strong voiced man, sang the whole time. He was assisted by young boys and girls, who sat at his feet, and beat time with the flat of their hand. These children also sang with the chief musical performer, who stood up the whole time.

At the end of each performance the spectators clapped and cheered.

'Budyeree caribberie,' (a good dance) they said using Eora words.

'That really was well worth seeing.' John Hunter said as the officers walked from the scene. Everyone agreed it had been a great experience.

****

However, not everyone was enjoying life at Sydney Cove. One night at the end of March, a daring escape took place by a group of convicts. The runaways were William Bryant, the colony's chief fisherman, his wife Mary, with their two small children, and seven other men.

Their planning had begun much earlier...

Due to his experience as a fisherman, William Bryant's job was to supervise the colony's fishing operations. But he'd been caught selling fish privately for his own profit and was publically punished with a hundred lashes. Despite his dishonesty, the Governor needed his skill for the colony's food supply, so he kept William in his role as chief fisherman. However, the couple had to move from their hut by the water into the settlement so William could be closely watched. Bryant simmered with anger about this treatment, and began planning his escape. Mary wanted to get away too and was willing to take great risks for her freedom. William started collecting and stashing useful equipment. The men who'd agreed to join him, hid stolen fishing nets, muskets, and tools. Mary collected and hid extra food, and gathered herbs from the bush, including leaves used to make tea.

When a Dutch ship visited Sydney Cove, Bryant managed to get information about the coast northward, helping him to plan their escape route. He also turned a series of other events to his advantage. He made sure the Governor's six-oared boat was in good condition and fitted with new sails, mast and oars. Once they had the necessary equipment, they had to wait for exactly the right time. It happened during the last week of March.

After the Dutch ship left, they knew there would be no ship left in the harbour capable of following them. If the weather stayed calm, that would be their best chance to make their escape.

March 28th was a moonless night and the wind and tide were perfect for a small boat to get down the harbour and out through the headlands into the Pacific Ocean. It was a nerve-racking few hours for Mary, William and the other seven men, as they silently made trips back and forth in the dark to load the boat.

Mary had to keep three-year-old Charlotte quiet as they crept to the wharf and bundled her into the boat.

'Shh, shh,' she signaled with her finger to her lips. 'We're all goin' in the Gov'nor's boat,' she whispered to her little girl.

She held her baby boy Emanuel close as she made her last trip to the waterfront. Her arms were aching from the loads she'd carried.

'I dropped some stuff, William,' she gasped, breathless from fear.

'Leave it – just get in the boat, luv,' William whispered tensely.

Finally, they pushed off from the wharf and rowed silently down the harbour, past the guards on the headland. They were finally in the open sea.

'We did it! We're free!' the escapees laughed and cheered.

Their absence wasn't discovered until early morning and by then they had been gone hours. The Governor's secretary recorded the details:

The escape was traced from Bryant's hut to the Point, and in the path were found a hand-saw, a scale, and four or five pounds of rice, scattered about in different places which they had dropped in their haste. On searching Bryant's hut, cavities under the boards were found, where he had hidden the compass and other items.

****

Once the escapees had made it into the Pacific Ocean, they sailed north, keeping the coast in sight whenever possible. Their plan was to head northward, to the Timor Sea where there were Dutch settlements. Once they got there, they intended to say they were shipwreck survivors. It was all cleverly planned.

At first the Bryants and their companions had been thrilled with their newfound freedom, but reality soon set in. They were lashed by storms, soaked by heavy rain and tossed by immense waves. Strong winds drove them out to sea where they had no sight of land for three weeks and then they suffered thirst and sunburn. All they had to eat then was raw rice. It was particularly distressing for Mary and the two little ones. But they had made their choice, and had to keep pressing on to their destination[14].

****

When their escape became public in Sydney, it created uproar. Their daring attempt inspired others to think about the possibility of freedom. No-one knew the Bryant's fate, but their venture was the topic of many conversations.

To prevent more escapes, Governor Phillip directed the guard on all boats would be increased and that small vessels could only be built under strict supervision. Without equipment or skills for sailing, anyone planning escape, would have to risk going inland.

Rumours began among the convicts that an escape route was possible beyond the mountains. The idea circulated that a legendary place existed in that direction; a place where no one had to work. Plans for mass escapes began being whispered as convicts went about their daily grind.

[14] Their destination was Timor, 3,000 miles or 5,000 kms from Sydney.

Chapter 32

Sydney Cove, April - May 1791

For Phillip, the inland was still a mystery he needed to solve. The colony had been settled for over three years and no one had conquered the mountains to the west of the settled areas. An expedition was planned to the river Tench had found west of Rose Hill, and if possible to the mountains beyond. He was looking forward to seeing what was out there.

Watkin Tench was also keen to go exploring again. He would be leaving the colony before the year's end and he wanted to make the most of the remaining time. He thought about earlier journeys inland and how much tougher they'd been than anyone expected.

Colbee and a younger native man named Ballooderry volunteered for the expedition, which included Governor Phillip, John White, Tench, Dawes and some soldiers, over twenty men altogether. The native men weren't familiar with the area west of Rose Hill but were keen for adventure. Before leaving they wanted to know how long the journey would be, and what food would be taken.

'Five days, Colbee,' Tench said showing the number with his hand. 'And we will take plenty of bread and meat,' he assured them.

Bennelong also wanted to join them but his strong-willed wife Barangaroo objected. Colbee made sure he was going by organising for his wife and baby to be cared for in Sydney while he was away.

'Daringa nanga pata Warran,' (Daringa will sleep and eat in Sydney) Colbee insisted, making arrangements for his wife.

With preparation complete, the group headed west from Rose Hill each carrying his backpack with provisions. As well as food, they carried blankets, cooking pots and tools. In addition to each one's load of twenty kilos, the men took extra shoes. Experience had shown the rough inland territory, with uneven stony ground and steep ridges, could rip the soles of leather boots in a short time.

William Dawes had the job of steering by compass, counting the number of paces and adding up the distance covered each day. Despite the Governor's disagreement with Dawes about the Botany Bay expedition, he knew the lieutenant's skill as a navigator. They were all aware of the danger of getting lost in the wilderness. Colbee and Ballooderry were going into unknown territory too, so they were impressed with the white men's tool for showing the way.

'Naa moro,' (to see the path) [15] Colbee said when Dawes explained how the compass worked.

During their first evening in the bush, as the men were chatting by the campfire, they heard voices a short distance away. Feeling the safety of their numbers, they asked Colbee to call out and invite whoever was there to come closer, to assure them of a friendly welcome and something to eat.

'Cooo-eee!' (Come here, I am here) Colbee called out the usual signal with a loud voice.

Eventually a man approached the campsite holding a bright burning stick and he, Colbee and Ballooderry introduced themselves. Colbee invited the stranger to join the group around the campfire but he hesitated after seeing the pale beings sitting there in their strange body coverings.

Who or what are the creatures?

[15] **Naa** means 'to see' and **mo-ro** means 'a path' Colbee explained.

Although the native men were strangers to each other, Colbee approached the visitor, took his hand and led him within the circle of white men. Watkin Tench described the scene:

> *By the light of the moon we were introduced to this gentleman, all our names being repeated by Colbee and Ballooderry, who said that we were Englishmen...that we came from the sea coast, and that we were travelling inland.*

'Budyeree,' (They are good men) Colbee assured the stranger.

After a long conversation between the native men, the visitor left with a gift of bread and meat. It was the first time the British explorers had spoken to a native man so far inland. It signaled a good start to the journey.

During the following days the group trekked over rough territory. The white men were exhausted but Colbee and Ballooderry walked on steadily and stayed in good spirits. As they trudged through swampy ground, climbed and slid down rock faces or tumbled into prickly undergrowth, Colbee and Ballooderry made fun of the white men whenever they stumbled. It was friendly banter and everyone knew it. However it soon became clear the native men didn't know where they were. When the group came to the river seen by Tench months earlier, the native men were surprised and delighted by it.

Despite the new sights, Colbee and Ballooderry were becoming tired of wandering around unfamiliar bush and living off the contents of backpacks. They were over swimming for ducks shot by the white men, and Ballooderry asked why *he* should be the one to fetch them, when it was the white men who'd eat them.

'He has a good point,' Tench said, hearing Ballooderry's protest.

The native men began asking when they'd be heading home, making it clear they wanted to go back to the comforts of Rose Hill.

'Rose Hill, budyeree,' (Rose Hill is good) Colbee said. 'At Rose Hill there's potato, cabbage, pumpkin, and fish.' He said he missed his wife and baby and asked again when they'd return to Rose Hill.

'Ngirigal (soon),' William Dawes answered, but avoided saying how many days.

While exploring along the river, they saw canoes at a distance, and later a native paddled toward the explorers. He took two stone hatchets and spears from his canoe and presented them to the Governor, who in return gave him two metal hatchets and some bread. The man looked at the bread, and looked at Colbee. He didn't know what to do with it, until Colbee demonstrated it was food.

'Bread budyeree pattane,' (Bread is good to eat) he told the man.

Soon another canoe approached with a younger man and a small boy. As they paddled parallel with the men walking on the bank, the explorers were surprised at the friendliness of the natives. They showed no sign of fear or distrust.

When the white men stopped to set up camp, they all sat around a fire and talked. Using signs, and with Colbee and Ballooderry's help, the explorers asked the local men questions. They learnt their diet included yams dug from the riverbank, root vegetables, fruit and berries, as well as meat. The man, whose name was Yellomundee, then asked about the white men. Tench wrote in his journal:

Colbee informed him who we were. He told him of our numbers at Sydney and Rose Hill and of the good things we have there. He listed potatoes, pumpkin, cabbages and many words that the man did not understand. But he nodded politely.

The native men stayed all night, sleeping around the fire. The little boy lay cradled in his father's arms.

Next morning the whole party had breakfast together. Then the white men watched a tree climbing demonstration by one of the native men. The performance made them stare in amazement.

With his hatchet he cut a small notch in the tree and fixed the big toe of his left foot, and sprung upwards, at the same time embracing the tree with his left arm. In an instant he cut a second notch for his right toe on the other side of the tree. And so alternately cutting on each side, he mounted to the height of twenty feet[16] as quickly as if he'd climbed a ladder, although the bark of the tree was quite smooth and slippery and perfectly straight.

To us it was a matter of astonishment, but to him it was sport, for while he was climbing, he kept talking to those below and laughing. He descended with as much ease and speed as he had raised himself.

[16] 20 feet = 6 metres.

Later that morning the Governor and his men shook hands with their new friends. Colbee and Ballooderry said goodbye with a nod of the head. As the two groups parted, Watkin Tench thought about the friendship and good humour they had shared.

****

As the explorers continued walking along the river the Governor had named *Nepean*, Colbee and Ballooderry made it clear they'd had enough of exploring. Tench gave the details in his journal:

> *We observed they were thoroughly sick of the journey, and whole-heartedly wished for its conclusion.*
>
> *'Where's Rose Hill?' they asked continually, with repeated questions about when we would get there.*

To Colbee and Ballooderry's delight, the Governor decided to head homeward the following day. The expedition had not reached the mountains but they had explored along the river at their base and they'd learnt about the native people living away from the coast.

The group reached Rose Hill at three o'clock in the afternoon, just as a boat was due to leave for Sydney Cove. When Colbee and Ballooderry heard this, they rushed ahead in order to catch it, rather than stay the night at Rose Hill with the rest of the explorers. They could not wait to tell Bennelong and the rest of their friends at Sydney Cove about all the things they had seen.

Chapter 33

Sydney Cove, June - December 1791

When Ballooderry arrived back in Sydney Cove, Nanberry and Boorong were eager to hear about his journey. He told them about the wide river he'd seen and the inland natives he'd met there.

Ballooderry was Boorong's older brother and he'd come to live in Sydney Cove after learning that she was there. The British officers described him as a fine young man and he was very popular with the settlers. Nanberry, now eleven years old, looked up to him as a mentor and friend. Governor Phillip thought highly of Ballooderry and they were on such friendly terms that he often ate meals at Government House, sometimes staying there for days. Phillip had even talked to Ballooderry about going to England one day.

Like others among his people, Ballooderry began to trade with the colonists, exchanging the extra fish he caught for bread, rice and salt meat. It was a practice that Governor Phillip had encouraged and hoped would become well established. Ballooderry was proud of his trading business and of his newly built canoe which he paddled between Sydney Cove and Rose Hill to deliver the fish.

One day in June something happened to destroy those happy arrangements, and the friendly bond between him and Governor Phillip. Ballooderry arrived at Rose Hill in the afternoon as usual with his supply of fish. He pulled his canoe onto the riverbank to a spot where it was hidden from view.

He knew some of the white people couldn't be trusted, despite the Governor's orders that native property must not be touched. This canoe was the first he'd built completely himself and it was his pride and joy.

After visiting some of the settlers in their huts and exchanging fish for other items, he returned to the river. As he reached the spot where he'd left his canoe, he saw it had been smashed to pieces. He was devastated.

By the time he reported the destruction to Phillip, he was in a rage. John Hunter described the scene when Ballooderry arrived to tell the Governor what had happened:

'Ghoólara murray,' (I am very angry) he said to the Governor.
'I will kill the men who did this!' he shouted.

He had his throwing-stick and several spears, and his hair, face, arms, and breast were painted red, which is a sign of great anger. It was with some difficulty that the Governor made him promise not to kill anyone, which he did after the Governor told him that he would kill those who had destroyed his canoe.

****

The convicts responsible for demolishing Ballooderry's canoe were caught and flogged. However the damage done by them was much more than the loss of a single canoe. After the incident, the native people stopped coming into Rose Hill. It was the end of trade for a while. And though Ballooderry had seen the white men flogged, he was not satisfied with the punishment. He decided he would deal with the issue according to his people's tribal law.

Some days after the incident, he speared and wounded a convict; someone who just happened to be passing by. Now it was Governor Phillip's turn to be angry. Ballooderry's action seemed completely unnecessary and because of it, the Governor banned him from the settlements.

For many who knew Ballooderry, the treatment seemed harsh. Watkin Tench discussed the disturbing incident with fellow officers.

'The truth is, some mischievous white men shamelessly destroyed Ballooderry's canoe and he revenged the damage on the first of our people he met unarmed,' Tench said.

'Well the Governor was shocked when he speared an innocent man. He thought Ballooderry was satisfied that the guilty men were flogged,' David Collins, Phillip's secretary added.

'I think Ballooderry believed it was up to *him* to punish the wrong done against him,' John Hunter said.

'Yes after he'd speared the convict he seemed to think the matter over, and settled in a fair and just way.' Tench added. 'In their own society, in similar cases, that's the custom it seems.'

'It's clear the Governor has a very high regard for Ballooderry but believes he can't allow him to throw spears as he pleases.'

'I have to say, I've never met a finer young man,' said David Collins. 'I think everyone regrets this unhappy situation.'

Hearing he'd been expelled from the settlement, Ballooderry stayed away. He liked the Governor but he didn't understand the white men's way of justice and punishment.

****

The whole sad story of the rift between Ballooderry and the Governor troubled eleven-year-old Nanberry. He didn't know what to think.

Nanberry enjoyed living at Sydney Cove. As the stepson of the colony's Chief Surgeon John White, he mixed with the leading people of the settlement. He'd quickly learnt and copied all the manners and habits that seemed important to the British people. He remembered to say, 'How do you do,' or 'Good afternoon,' when he met important people like Mrs Macarthur at the Governor's house. He used his knife and fork the way the white people did, and when he dined at the Governor's table he remembered to wipe his hands on a napkin and not on his trousers. He felt important, and he knew the British people were doing their best to look after him. Most of all, he knew John White, his Be-anna, wanted him to be happy and he was very attached to him.

Despite all this, he often felt the pull of his own culture, and returned to play in the bush around the harbour with other native children. He couldn't wait to kick off his shoes and feel the sand between his toes as he played on the beach, or strip off his shirt and trousers to dive into the cool water of Sydney Cove.

He still planned to be a warrior one day, so whenever he had the chance, he played with Eora boys his age. They made spears from sticks or strong reeds, and cut thick sheets of bark into shields. They spent hours aiming and warding off each other's spears as they'd seen their elders do.

Being years older than Nanberry, Ballooderry had taught him things about his culture he hadn't learnt while growing up in Sydney Cove. They'd gone fishing together whenever John White was away or busy.

****

After Ballooderry was barred from the settlement, he was seen one day near the town and a band of soldiers was sent to bring him in. Nanberry was at the Governor's house when the order was given and the boy decided he must prevent it. He quickly took off into the bush along a short-cut to warn his friend that soldiers were on their way. John Hunter recorded the incident in his journal:

> *A party of soldiers were ordered to secure Ballooderry, but before they got sight of him, the boy Nanberry heard what was planned and left the place. He ran into the woods and stripping himself, joined the natives, and put them on their guard.*
>
> *When he returned, he hid in a bush and saw the Governor go past with some officers. Later he asked where the Governor and the soldiers were going. Being told he laughed and said they were too late, for the natives had gone.*

Nanberry felt confused when his loyalty was pulled this way and that.

****

Bennelong tried to act as go-between and to end the disagreement between the Governor and Ballooderry who'd once been good friends. But Phillip believed he could not excuse the young man's attack on an innocent, unarmed person. That was, until several months later when he learnt that Ballooderry was very ill. Then he immediately sent the doctor to see him. Surgeon John White found Ballooderry suffering a high fever.

'Is Gov'nor still angry?' Ballooderry asked when he saw John White.

Stories of Life at Sydney Cove

One look at Ballooderry told the doctor he needed to be treated in the hospital, and reported his condition to the Governor.

'No, I am not angry now,' Phillip said when he heard the doctor's account. 'He must be brought to the hospital as soon as possible.' All issues were forgotten other than Ballooderry's recovery. John Hunter recorded the Governor's reaction when he saw the young man looking so sick:

> *The governor took him by the hand, promising that when he was recovered he should stay with him again. Poor Ballooderry appeared to be very ill, and went with the surgeon to the hospital.*

John White used all his skills to help Ballooderry. Then he stepped aside for Bennelong to try a method to cure his friend:

> *Bennelong applied his mouth to those parts of his patient's body which he thought were affected, breathing strongly on them, and singing. At times he waved some boughs dipped in water, holding one in each hand, treating him with much attention and friendship.*

A day later a Koradji (a man of special power) arrived in Sydney Cove from the harbour's north shore to see Ballooderry. When he came to the hospital, John White stood back as the Koradji performed a healing ritual.

But in the end, all the remedies in the world could not save their much-loved Ballooderry. When he died later that night, it was agreed between Bennelong, his people and Phillip that Ballooderry should be buried in the Governor's garden.

His body was wrapped in the English jacket he'd loved wearing, and he was placed in a canoe with his spears and fishing gear beside him. Bennelong and Colbee took great care positioning his body, trimming shrubs and branches to make sure the sun's rays reached the burial site. Then working together the young man's friends, both black and white, lowered him into his grave and filled it.

Nanberry, now twelve, witnessed the sad event with images flowing through his mind, memories of fishing and laughing with his friend. He and Ballooderry had exchanged names to signify their close bond, but now he must give up the name and not mention it. Now his friend was gone.

Boorong was there, mourning the death of her older brother. She'd learnt only the previous year that he had survived the smallpox epidemic. And later he'd come to live in Sydney Cove, often staying at the Governor's house. She thought about his trading business and his many friendships. Everything had gone well for him until his canoe had been smashed...

'No point thinking that now,' she told herself. 'Today it's goodbye.'

Ballooderry's father Maugoran, stood quietly watching as his people and the British joined together in the burial of his son. David Collins wrote about the occasion later:

> *When Ballooderry, a very fine lad died among us, I saw the tears streaming silently down the cheek of his father Maugoran...He stood alone and still, a silent observer of all that was doing about his deceased son. He was a perfect picture of deep sorrow.*

Chapter 34

Sydney Cove, June - December 1791

When Lieutenant George Johnston returned to Sydney Cove from his one-year-posting on Norfolk Island, he knew important decisions had to be made. His tour of duty in the colony would soon be over. A third fleet of ships had arrived with news that *HMS Gorgon* was on its way to take the First Fleet marines home to England.

The idea of returning to his mother country was very appealing. It had been a tough few years serving in the New South Wales colony; much harder than he'd imagined. He really wanted to return to England, but there was a lot to consider.

George's life had changed. He was a family man now. He had a relationship with Esther Abrahams, and as well as the care of her daughter, they had their own dear boy George, now eighteen months old. On top of that, he'd just heard from Esther that they were expecting another baby.

He wanted Hetty, as he fondly called Esther, to be part of his future but he had to keep reminding himself that she was a convict. She was a sensible, caring woman but she was still serving her seven-year-sentence. She couldn't return to England with him. She had to stay in the colony and serve her time.

Besides family considerations, George Johnston knew there would be advantages to staying in the colony. There was the prospect of further promotion and the promise of a large land grant.

So despite his homeland having a strong pull and the colony still lacking the comforts of civilised life, he decided he'd stay in New South Wales. He and Esther would build a future together.

Sydney Cove had changed. It was a very different place to the settlement he and Esther had left sixteen months earlier. They'd gone to Norfolk Island on Governor Phillip's orders, before the food crisis had reached its worst. While there, they'd heard reports of events in Sydney Cove, but they hadn't witnessed the dramas. They hadn't been there for the arrival of the Second Fleet bringing desperately needed provisions, news from England and hundreds more convicts. They'd missed the Governor's spearing, his reunion with Bennelong and the natives' first willing visit to the settlement.

On his return to Sydney Cove, George Johnston saw many improvements in the township but the most noticeable change was the large number of Eora families who now lived there. Many Aboriginal people now stayed in the homes of white settlers as part of their extended families. When the men met privately, Johnston raised the topic of the Governor's cultural project, in which he had played a part in the kidnap of Arabanoo in 1788.

'All your effort for friendly contact with the native people seems to have worked at last, Sir,' said George Johnston.

'We've had our ups and downs and there are decisions I regret. But yes, I'm very pleased to have goodwill at last,' replied Phillip.

'Yes I'm sure, Sir.'

'My problem at the moment is lazy thieving convicts. They steal food from the gardens of other hardworking people. I've had the offenders chained together and ordered to wear thick iron collars in the hope of preventing further thefts, so we'll see.'

'That should stop them,' said Johnston, imagining the punishment.

'Another problem is that convicts are still stealing natives' fishing equipment,' Phillip continued. 'One of the culprits was caught in the act and I had him flogged in the presence of many native people here at Sydney Cove. I wanted to demonstrate again that I didn't approve of the thefts.'

'That was surely the best thing, Sir.' Johnston nodded in agreement.

'Mm...but it had the opposite effect to what I'd hoped. All the natives watching the flogging, both men and women, disagreed with the punishment. In fact, they had sympathy for the man! Colbee's wife Daringa, stood there shedding tears for the convict. And Bennelong's wife, our Barangaroo, grabbed a stick, marched over to the man with the whip in his hand and started hitting *him* with it!'

Phillip and Johnston both laughed, seeing the funny side to the story.

'Well Sir, it's good that open communication is possible at last,' said Johnston, still seeing the lighter side of the incident.

'Not all the Eora have the same vision though,' Phillip continued on a serious note. 'Some, like the man Pemulwuy, seem to consider us their enemies and make a point of attacking our people whenever they can. You'll remember, Pemulwuy was the man who speared my servant McEntire?' Phillip asked, and Johnston nodded.

'In fact,' Phillip continued. 'I've received word that a large party of natives almost destroyed a hut belonging to a settler not far from Rose Hill. He may have been killed but for the well-timed arrival of another settler with a musket.'

'Do you think Pemulwuy was behind it, Sir?

'I'm not sure. It's a dilemma,' Phillip replied gazing into the distance.

There were issues surrounding Pemulwuy's stand that Phillip found challenging.

****

The ships that brought news that *HMS Gorgon* was on its way to take the marines back to England, also carried instructions for Phillip. The British government had made it clear they didn't want ex-convicts returning to England once their sentences ended. They instructed Phillip to offer them incentives to stay in the colony. The Governor therefore assembled the people whose sentences were close to ending, and gave them their options:

'Those of you who wish to become settlers in this country, will be given every encouragement. I'll give details of this option later... Those of you who wish to return to England when you're free, may do so. No obstacle will be put in your way to leaving on any ship that will give you passage...'

There was a murmur among the assembled convicts. Many of them longed to return to their families, but didn't have money or any means of paying for the voyage. They waited for the Governor to continue.

'However, you must not expect assistance from the Government to that end. You will have to make your own arrangements.'

The buzz of the crowd became an uproar as convicts protested the injustice of the arrangement.

'That's not fair. Who of us can manage that?'
'So we get a free ride out 'ere, but 'ave to pay to go back 'ome.'
'I don't wanna be a farmer! It's not right!' someone shouted.

'Those who don't want to become farmers can work on various government projects in return for weekly rations,' Phillip added.

He then turned to those who wished to settle as farmers:

'The following conditions are offered to those who decide to settle: You will be allotted thirty acre plots of ground around the area we have called Rose Hill. I am now changing the name of that town to

Parramatta, which is the name given to that place by the natives.' The Governor paused for the new information to sink in.

'Married couples will receive fifty acre lots. You'll be clothed and fed from the public store for eighteen months from the time you settle. You'll receive tools and each of you will receive a number of animals as can be spared. In addition you'll be supplied with grain and seeds to plant on your land.'

****

That afternoon Sydney Cove was abuzz with conversation about the Governor's speech. Old Dot visited Henry and Susannah Kable.

'I know you two will be staying here, but I'm goin' first chance.'

'Don't you still 'ave a year of ye time to serve, Dot?' Henry asked.

'Yes but that'll give me time to work me plan. I'm 'oping due to me old age, they'll take pity an' just send me.' She said with a chuckle.

'We'd never get a chance like this in England,' Henry Kable said to his wife. 'I know you miss your country, I do too. But just think...'

'I know our children can live better 'ere, so this is where I want to stay,' said Susannah.

'By the way,' said Dot changing the topic. 'Did you hear from Esther Abrahams how young Elizabeth Hayward's goin' on Norfolk Island?'

'As a matter of fact I did ask Esther, and she said the lass is goin' well and stayin' out of trouble. She's still got a few years of her time to go, but she's doin' alright on Norfolk Island for now. Same for young John Hudson I hear. He's stayin' out o' trouble too.'

****

After the Governor's announcement about their limited options, some convicts began planning to secretly stow themselves on ships sailing for England. Some began plotting their escape to the imaginary place said to exist beyond the mountains. Others decided that the Governor's offer of a land grant sounded like a good deal. The Governor's secretary recorded the sites of the various grants:

> *The governor has now chosen situations for his settlers, and fixed them on their different allotments.*
>
> *Twelve convicts, whose terms of transportation had expired, he placed on land at the foot of a hill named Prospect Hill, west from Parramatta; fifteen others were placed on land in a district north-east of Parramatta named The Ponds.*

One of the settlers who received a land grant at The Ponds was Matthew Everingham, a convict whose seven-year sentence had just ended. He had no experience as a farmer but wanted to give it a go. He was determined to prove he'd changed his ways.

Seven years earlier...

At the age of fifteen, Matthew worked in London as an attorney's clerk, delivering messages between different law offices in the city. He was arrested for stealing two law books belonging to an attorney and trying to sell them. He admitted his guilt, saying in court that he was 'in great distress'. The judge sentenced him to seven years transportation but he spent years in prison before the First Fleet sailed. By the time he arrived in Sydney Cove he had less than three years left of his sentence. He was relieved when the Governor sent him to work for the store supervisor, because he could read and write.

****

When Matthew moved to his plot of land near Parramatta, he was twenty-two and recently married. At first, life did not go well for Matthew and his wife Elizabeth. They both came from cities and had no experience with farming. But despite the obstacles, they decided they'd give it their very best effort.

'When things are at their worst, they can only get better.' Matthew always said to himself and his wife when things became difficult.

****

By late 1791, the township of Parramatta had become well established. A barge transported goods and people regularly to and from Sydney Cove. A wide track led from the wharf all the way to the hill where the Governor's house overlooked the other buildings. Phillip stayed there whenever he needed to check on work that was underway. Brick huts for convict workers lined each side of the main street. Each building housed a minimum of ten convicts and had room for a vegetable garden. Barracks for the soldiers, a guardhouse and storehouses had been built, and recently a house had been finished for Reverend Johnson. The building of a town hall with a market place, and a new hospital were planned. The settlers' farms were in some cases a few hours walk from the township.

A view of the Governor's house at Parramatta

Before the year ended, more than a thousand white settlers had moved westward to the town of Parramatta and its surrounding area, in addition to the hundreds already there.

****

When Pemulwuy, the native warrior, heard that many more white people had moved inland, he knew something must be done. He had no idea of their actual numbers, but the effect of the white settlers on the land of his people was sadly obvious wherever they went. The places now being cleared and developed by the white men were areas where his people had dug yams, gathered edible ferns and other greens, and where animals had been hunted. These food sources were important when fish was scarce. The land the British had built on, were places his people had visited to collect material for canoes and fishing gear.

Pemulwuy thought the white men's clearing methods were not right or reasonable. He believed there must be a response to the displacement of his people, and he would be the one to lead it.

He knew his people had superior knowledge and practices in bush survival. They could use those skills to their advantage to stand up to the white man's powerful weapons. The settlers were very dependent on the produce they farmed so attacks on their crops would send a message that not all native people would watch passively as their land was taken. But he would not rush things. He would continue to build support among his people to defend their land and their rights.

****

Meanwhile, during the spring of 1791, Bennelong and Barangaroo welcomed their first baby into the world; a little girl named Dilboong, meaning 'bell bird'. Bennelong had wanted his baby to be born at Government House but when the time came, Barangaroo chose a private place outside the settlement where she placed her newborn baby on a soft, specially prepared paperbark blanket.

While Barangaroo lived at Sydney Cove her energetic personality had been impossible to ignore, so when she died suddenly after the birth of her baby girl, it came as a shock to everyone.

Her grieving husband asked Governor Phillip to find a suitable white woman to look after his baby. From his first months at Sydney Cove, Bennelong had given the Governor the special title 'Be-anna' (father). Now the Governor learnt this title also brought family responsibility. Bennelong explained it meant he shared the care and upbringing of his child. David Collins, the governor's secretary wrote the details:

> *Bennelong told us at the death of his wife that the care of his infant daughter Dil-boong went to his friend Governor Phillip, telling him that he was to become the Be-anna or father of his little girl.*

Barangaroo's funeral took place in the Governor's garden with Governor Phillip, Doctor John White and other officers standing alongside the grieving Bennelong and his relatives. She was wrapped in an English blanket, with her basket of fishing gear placed beside her.

When little Dilboong died shortly after her mother, she was also buried in the Governor's garden.

Chapter 35

Sydney Cove, November - December 1791

The arrival of a third fleet of ships brought more dramas for the Governor. The newly arrived convicts made complaints about cruelty and ill-treatment on their voyage. They said they hadn't received enough food, and their pale faces and frail bodies showed they'd been crammed below deck in terrible conditions. The Governor was angry that the ship's masters had withheld rations and used the space meant for convicts to store items they planned to sell to the settlers at Sydney Cove. Phillip intended reporting the matter to the British government.

Meanwhile the ships' masters, knowing the settlers had been living without basic needs for some time, sold their goods for the highest possible profit. What they didn't sell in Sydney they knew they could trade in India or China on their return to England.

****

Many of the recently arrived convicts were restless and rebellious. Some were Irish prisoners believing their sentences were illegal. None of them wanted to be in the remote colony and constantly talked of escape. Others, whose sentences had ended, were also depressed by their situation. They didn't want to stay and work in in the colony. Stories of a better place somewhere overland became attractive, and risky plans to reach the imaginary site began.

In November, settlers working in their field near Parramatta saw a group of twenty convicts heading into the bush carrying clothes, tools and blankets. When the settlers asked where they were going, the group answered in unison:

'To China!'

A search party was sent after them but they got away. Within a week however some of the group staggered back into Parramatta exhausted. Others were found starving in the surrounding bush. When questioned about their escape, they admitted they'd believed China was easy to reach, being on the other side of a river. The Governor's secretary recorded the incident.

> *Thirteen of those who escaped were brought back in a terrible state, half naked, and worn out with hunger. Some had survived by sucking on flowering shrubs and wild berries of the woods. They were a picture of misery that seemed enough to deter others from the same stupidity.*

The horror stories, and even the skeletons found surrounded by shoes and other belongings, didn't stop others trying to escape.

Old Dot tut-tutted at their foolishness.

'None of us First Fleeters ever tried anythin' so stupid, did we? But this place is full of strangers now, not like the old days when ye knew everyone's name...It's all changed... Tryin' to get to China! Even I know ye can't walk there!' Dot said to Susannah Kable.

'Actually there was Ann Smith,' said Susannah thinking back.

'Do you remember, Dot? She came on the *Lady Penrhyn* with us, and she escaped a few days after we landed...back in 1788.'

'Oh yes, I'd forgotten all about 'er...we never did find out what 'appened, to 'er, did we?'

'No, I think her story will stay a mystery.'

****

By the end of the year, forty-four men and nine women were missing from the settlements. The Governor's secretary gave his report.

> *Among that number were those wandering in the woods trying to get on to the path to China! Many of that number died miserably. Others found their way back after some weeks and reported the fate of their companions, looking starving and exhausted themselves.*

Watkin Tench went to the hospital at Parramatta to interview four men who were recovering from their ordeal:

> *I asked these men if they really supposed it possible to reach China. They answered that they were certainly made to believe that a large river existed which separated this country from China, and that when they crossed it, they'd find themselves among a copper-coloured people who would treat them kindly.*

The settlers and officers at Parramatta, who saw the bleeding feet, sunken cheeks and injured bodies of the returned escapees, called them the 'Chinese Travellers'.

As time went by, convicts began inventing tools to find their way through the bush. There were wild ideas put forward of ways to improve their chances of escape. One of these ideas was a compass drawn on a piece of paper! The officers thought it was a great joke that convicts would rely on such an invention.

One of them told the story of a convict, who'd been brought into the settlement after roving about lost in the bush for days.

'He was in search of a road to China and he had written instructions telling him to keep the sun on a certain side of his body.'

'Oh yes I think I've heard this story before,' laughed Watkin Tench.

'After wandering about for days and his food almost gone, he had the sense to turn back. Hearing gunshot at a distance, he walked toward it, calling out at the top of his voice. But night came before he met anyone. Being exhausted he took some flour from his pocket, sprinkled it into water and drank it, before collapsing.

In the morning, he pushed on trying to get to the place where he'd heard gunshot and after yelling for hours someone finally answered. His rescuer, who was a settler, took him to his house, fed him and brought him into the town.

On being questioned about how he found his way back, the man said that the paper compass he'd been given was no help, so he kept his face toward the direction the sun came from. Otherwise, he said, he'd have died as he had no food for two days, except a bit of flour and water.'

'A compass drawn on paper! How could anyone believe that?'

'When you're desperate, I guess you try anything,' said Tench.

It was easy for the officers and marines to criticise the lengths some convicts went to in their quest for freedom. Their own escape from the colony was close on the horizon; they'd soon be going home to England. *HMS Gorgon*, the ship that would take them back, had arrived! They could begin packing to leave.

Soon they'd be sailing across the great expanse of ocean to the opposite end of the earth once again. This time however, they were heading to the familiar sights of England, to the comforts of civilisation and the waiting arms of their families.

Chapter 36

Sydney Cove, December 1791

Elizabeth Macarthur stood amid the crowd by the wharf waving her goodbyes with a heavy heart. *HMS Gorgon* was leaving on its return voyage to England with many of the First Fleet marines and officers aboard. With no female friends in the colony, the officers had become her social network. She'd miss the gatherings and musical evenings, with her husband John and his colleagues, chatting and singing songs from home.

Lieutenants Watkin Tench and William Dawes had gone on board. She would miss her conversations with the likable Mr Tench, and with the thoughtful, intelligent Mr Dawes. He had sparked her interest in the plants and flowers around Sydney Cove and taught her about the southern stars at his observatory. With him no longer living there, she would have no reason to walk the track to the observatory. She pictured lonely days ahead but comforted herself with the thought that free settlers would arrive in the colony soon.

****

From the deck of *HMS Gorgon*, Watkin Tench looked ashore to the crowd waving them goodbye. Some of the First Fleet officers were staying in Sydney Cove. The Reverend had agreed to a few more years in the colony, as had Chief Surgeon John White.

Tench saw many Eora faces among the crowd, people he considered his friends. He respected them and he'd learnt a lot from them.

What an amazing four years he'd had since landing at Botany Bay!

He vividly remembered his first meeting with the natives: the day he'd slowly walked up the beach toward them, holding the hand of a seven-year-old child. He recalled the gentleness shown by an old native man toward the little boy as he'd come forward and laid his hand on the child's hat, felt his clothes and muttered in astonishment at the whiteness of the boy's skin.

On a personal level, Watkin Tench had fond memories of Arabanoo, Bennelong, Barangaroo and many others. He'd recorded every fascinating event in his journal, but like most of the officers aboard *HMS Gorgon*, he was ready to leave Sydney Cove.

William Dawes, on the other hand, wanted to stay. He had many friends among the Eora, but he'd had a particularly close friendship with a young woman Patyegarang, or Patye as he called her. He had spent the happiest days of his life on the quiet headland at his observatory learning about her ways, her language and her people.

Dawes had seen the impact of the white settlements on the native people, especially inland where settlement had spread without consultation. He sympathised with their issues. He'd criticised some of the Governor's decisions and knew he had his disapproval. Now he was on his way back to England. Standing beside his friend Tench aboard *HMS Gorgon*, William Dawes felt empty and helpless. He was leaving the colony forever. He'd never see Patye again.

Chapter 37

Sydney Cove, January - November 1792

More challenges arrived for Governor Phillip during the early months of 1792. A reduction in rations was necessary again, convicts continued to escape into the wilderness in search of 'China', and the Governor had his own health concerns. Not a day went by that he didn't suffer pain in his side from an unknown cause. So when *Royal Admiral* sailed into Sydney Harbour in October with more convicts, supplies and letters, Governor Phillip was pleased to read news of a personal nature. He'd received permission to quit the colony and return to England to attend to his health.

Believing his news would create uncertainty, he waited some weeks before announcing it publicly. Phillip knew his departure would bring change. It would be a time of transition for everyone.

He was very aware that after he left, the colony would need strong men as leaders. He had urged Lieutenant George Johnston to stay as Commanding Officer of the New South Wales Corps for a further term. Fortunately he'd accepted and enlisted marines to stay under his command. Phillip had also offered incentives for marines to remain in the colony as farmers, and more than fifty had seized the opportunity. They saw the benefits of settling in New South Wales.

****

As Phillip's time as governor came to its end, three young women were looking to their future at Sydney Cove with positive outlooks.

Elizabeth Macarthur, Esther Abrahams and Susannah Kable had very different backgrounds, but they also had a lot in common.

Esther and Susannah were still serving time as convicts, but Elizabeth as the wife of a soldier, was a free woman. However, each of the women had endured the same trials since arriving in the colony and each of them could look forward to increasing wealth and success for her family.

Each woman had arrived in Sydney Cove with a very young child. Esther Abrahams and Susannah Kable had suffered the hardship of caring for a baby below deck during their voyage as convicts. But Elizabeth Macarthur had also experienced terrible conditions aboard a transport ship of the Second Fleet. She'd grieved the death of her baby girl on the voyage and almost lost her husband to an illness that had left him weak.

After arriving in Sydney Cove, each mother had bravely adjusted to her new situation, caring for an infant while living in a primitive hut in strange surroundings. They'd all adjusted to the different weather conditions: the heat, the violent storms that visited the Sydney area and the hot summer winds that felt like the blast of an oven. Each woman had adapted to her new environment, accepting that spiders, insects and other creatures were part of it. They had all boldly met the challenges.

By the end of 1792, Esther Abrahams, the Londoner convicted for stealing a roll of lace, had reason to feel satisfied with her situation. When she and baby Roseanna went aboard *Lady Penrhyn* six years earlier, she'd wondered what life held for them. But she'd caught the attention of Lieutenant George Johnston and her life had taken a turn for the better. Though she couldn't forget she was still a convict, Esther Abrahams had security. George was a devoted father to their son, he'd been offered promotion and he'd soon receive a generous land grant.

Susannah Kable, the convict whose story had made British newspapers with her tale of forced separation from her baby, also had reason to be content. Her husband Henry had continued in the Governor's good favour and he'd been appointed as a constable[17]. They had a comfortable home in Sydney Cove and they were already building wealth and a good future for their children.

Life was looking rosy for Elizabeth Macarthur. Her husband's military career looked very promising and they'd soon receive a large parcel of land at Parramatta. She missed the lush green fields of England, but she also loved the wild beauty of her new land. She'd written to a friend in England that she was 'abundantly content'. She shared her husband's vision for the colony and could see the possibilities New South Wales offered.

All three women would remain in the colony for the rest of their lives, never seeing their homeland again. Despite their different backgrounds, Elizabeth Macarthur, Esther Abrahams and Susannah Kable would each have large colonial families who would play a significant role in the progress of the colony. The Macarthurs would become leaders in the wool industry, while the Kables would become traders and ship owners. Esther would later marry George Johnston and their children would become explorers and land developers. Of course they didn't know this at the end of 1792, but they had confidence about their prospects.

---

[17] constable = policeman

Chapter 38

Sydney Cove, December 1792

Governor Phillip read the report he was preparing to take to England. His time in the settlement had drawn to a close. Overall, he was satisfied with the progress that had been made. At Parramatta, farms were producing steadily. The time was in sight when settlers would be able to support their families from their farms.

Sydney was expanding at a steady pace with more buildings of brick and stone. The white population of the colony had increased to around four thousand and there were more Eora among them than ever. In the harbour, shipping activity was growing. Government boats were being built and whaling ships from America and Europe were visiting Sydney. A new phase was beginning.

'There are opportunities here for men with vision,' Phillip thought. 'Men like the convict builder James Bloodworth, and others.'

In Sydney there was hardly a building that hadn't benefitted from Bloodworth's ideas and input. Phillip had appointed him Master Builder and since offered him a free passage to England as a reward. Fortunately he'd chosen to stay in the colony.

There were other convicts who'd been determined to put their past behind them. Phillip's thoughts went to James Ruse, the farmer. He'd shown that convicts could become self-supporting, and that farming was possible in the colony. He and his wife had inspired others to have a go, even when the odds didn't look promising.

Matthew Everingham was another example of success. At the age of fifteen he'd made the unfortunate mistake of stealing. But he was doing alright now. He'd shown Phillip a letter he'd written to Samuel Shepherd, the attorney whose law books he'd stolen. Shepherd had kept in touch with Matthew to support him when his family and friends had turned their backs on him after his arrest.

Matthew wanted to share his achievements with the man who had encouraged and believed in him:

To Samuel Shepherd Esq.

Ponds, Parramatta New South Wales
12th October, 1792

Most Honoured Sir,

In July last year my time expired and I went to see His Excellency. I chose to turn settler on condition of being supported eighteen months in supplies and clothing. Fifty acres was measured for my wife and I.

The first six months everything seemed to go against me. My crop failed, my baby daughter died, and my wife was very ill. Without supplies from England, the whole colony was almost starving.

This was bad encouragement for a young beginner but I have now settled 15 months and my little farm thank God promises pretty well and my wife is now healthy. I have five acres of corn, one of English wheat, half of barley, pumpkins, melons etc. in abundance. I have pigs, some chickens and a hive of bees.

In three months, I think I will be able to maintain my family independent of the public store, and do the best for myself.

Your very unworthy humble servant,

Matthew James Everingham

People like the Everinghams had proved the doubters wrong. They hadn't given up when the going got tough.

As Phillip sat reading his report, David Collins came into the room.

'I've been thinking about what's been achieved here,' Phillip said to his secretary. 'Remember when we first arrived, Collins? There were so many bewildering sights and obstacles to overcome.'

'Yes Sir I do. We landed in a wilderness not knowing what to expect. At the time, I thought how peaceful the little cove was...then the sound of our axes and hammers had shattered the stillness.'

'I remember,' said Phillip picturing the scene. 'We endured a lot in those early days. At times I wondered if we'd survive,' he added. 'But I have no doubt now that Sydney will be an important place one day. Trade will develop and other opportunities will follow. The children of convicts are in a good position to profit from it.'

'As long as food production keeps up with the growing population, I agree Sir, the colony has a future,' Collins added.

'You know the choices people make always intrigues me Collins,' Phillip continued. 'Some made a success of their situation here while others continued their same old ways and suffered for it.'

'Their reactions have varied,' Collins agreed. 'In the same month Ruse announced he could support himself on his farm, William Bryant and his group fled the colony by boat.'
'Yes, they had very different attitudes,' agreed Phillip.

'Anyway Sir, if there's nothing else, I'll head off,' Collins ended.

When he left, Phillip recalled the Bryant's story. He'd received news that all eleven escapees, including the two small children, had actually made it 3,000 miles[18] to Timor in the stolen fishing-boat. Incredibly the journey had taken them just under ten weeks but they'd endured storms, thirst, starvation and sunstroke. On arrival in Timor, they'd posed as shipwreck survivors and for a while their story was believed and they were treated kindly. But soon a slip of the

[18] 3,000 miles = 5,000 kms

tongue aroused suspicion and the true details of their escape came out. Then they were imprisoned by the Dutch Governor of Timor until they were handed over to the next English ship bound for Britain. After all their careful planning and incredible suffering, the escapees were on their way to England to be thrown into prison again. Phillip wondered what the final outcome would be for them.

His mind turned to the other lives that had been changed by Sydney Cove: the convicts, the Aboriginal families, and all those who'd stay when he left for England.

There were the teachers Isabella and William Richardson who'd set up a school for the children of convicts and marines. When the Reverend Johnson had praised them and suggested their appointment as teachers, Phillip had happily agreed. Now there was a school in Sydney, and one at Parramatta. The convict children were taught for free but marines paid a small charge. Phillip smiled at the thought that those who'd arrived in the colony on the lowest rung of society, now received a free education. They wouldn't get that in England.

One student, Harry Kable, had been a baby when his convict parents arrived in Sydney Cove. Now he was six and a promising little fellow with a sister and a baby brother. His parents had begun their education too. When Henry and Susannah had married in 1788, they could only sign with an X. Now they were learning to write.

Phillip knew many convicts longed to return to England. Dorothy Handland, the convict listed in ships' records as eighty-two, had only months of her seven-year sentence remaining. Many had doubted she'd survive life in the colony, but she'd plodded on and was still determined to go back to the 'old country'. He would organise for her to get back to her homeland.

****

Phillip looked across the harbour, to the opposite shore where the smoke of native fires drifted upward like fingers of mist. He imagined the families gathered around their campsites, some repairing their hunting spears, others preparing food as children played nearby. He'd often watched Eora children at their favourite game: lined up, each with a stick in hand, trying to be the first to hit a ball as it rolled along the row of children. He thought about the native people and their varied reactions to the white settlement.

How would they meet the challenges they were now facing?

He thought of Bennelong, his cheery, open-minded friend, who also maddened him at times. He knew Bennelong wanted the best for his people. He'd tried to find a middle-ground to improve the relationship between his culture and the settlers whose lifestyles were so different. In the end he decided the advantages the British offered, outweighed the disadvantages. Phillip admired Bennelong. He was a true diplomat.

Then there were those with Pemulwuy's view who were making it clear they saw no benefits in the white man's culture. They disliked the changes brought on their people and their land. Over previous months, settlers at Parramatta had complained of attacks on their crops, and Phillip suspected Pemulwuy was behind the activity.

What would become of Pemulwuy?
Would others continue his fight?

Nanberry and Boorong, the young smallpox survivors, still lived in Sydney Cove despite leaving for a short time. Boorong had become restless after learning that members of her family were alive. Seeing more of her people had made her miss their way of living. She said she wanted to marry among her own society and had left the Reverend's household to live with them.

Phillip read an account of that period:

Some days ago, a canoe with several young people came to the cove, and the girl who lived with the clergyman's wife joined them, and was very keen to go away with them.

So she was let go and allowed to take all her clothes with her, and told that whenever she chose to come and see her friends, whatever she wanted would be given her.

The next day she was seen naked in a canoe, but she put on a petticoat before she joined the clergyman and some others who went to visit her. She appeared pleased with her liberty.

Nanberry was with the party that went to see her, and he also wished to stay with the natives all night so he was left behind. But the next morning he returned to the surgeon, with whom he lived, and did not seem inclined to go away again.

Boorong later returned to Sydney Cove and had since seemed content to live across both cultures, coming and going as she pleased.

Nanberry was still part of John White's family. He happily wore English clothes and adapted to the white people's ways but he often spent days with his Eora friends. He clearly enjoyed the campfires of native families, and felt the appeal of their lifestyle. Phillip knew Nanberry would soon reach an age when he'd want to go through the initiation ceremony of his people, involving the removal of a front tooth. Nanberry looked to Bennelong and Colbee as role models; they were warriors among his people. Phillip also knew Nanberry was close to John White, the man who'd raised him from a boy of nine. But Surgeon White wouldn't stay in the colony forever. The hard-working doctor was worn out, and wanted to return to England.

Could Nanberry and Boorong keep their own heritage strong while successfully living as part of the colonial world?

At times, it had been difficult to prove the benefits of the British justice system to the natives who lived in the white settlements. They strongly disagreed with flogging and hanging. Phillip had tried to show the value of British culture in other ways, through housing, farming and education. He must believe and be confident they would see the benefits with time. He was leaving the colony, but his role in promoting British society was not over yet. That was where Bennelong came in. He was sailing to England with Phillip!

Bennelong wanted to go to Britain; a place that none of his people had seen. He wanted to learn more about what they had to offer.

Sydney Cove 1790s

Aboard *Atlantic*, 11th December 1792

Governor Phillip stood on board *Atlantic*, the ship that was taking him to England and looked across at Bennelong. He felt fondness for this young man who had given him so many headaches! How would he cope in England? Phillip knew Bennelong, and the other young adventurer Yemerawane who'd also volunteered for the journey, didn't realise how far they were going. He had tried to explain the distance, but they had no idea how long they'd be away from their homeland. The changes they'd face would be immense: the weather, the language, the people, the landscape. The sights they'd see would be mind-boggling.

If Bennelong had been impressed with the faded red jackets of the officers, what would he think when he saw English gentlemen in silk waistcoats and top hats, and ladies in their fancy dresses? He'd been delighted with the little brick house built for him at Sydney Cove, so what would he think when he saw the King's palace? What would he make of shops stocked with every kind of toy imaginable? Bennelong had thought the carts used in the settlement were amazing, so what would he think when he rode in an elegant carriage pulled by a team of horses? He'd thought the wharf at Sydney Cove impressive, so what would he think of London Bridge?

London Bridge 1790s

Stories of Life at Sydney Cove

****

Bennelong was trembling. It had been an upsetting farewell with his family and friends. He knew, had his beloved Barangaroo still been alive, she wouldn't agree with him going to the land of the British. But it was something he wanted to do and his excitement had been difficult to hide. He stood on deck with Governor Phillip waving to the crowd on shore until they were dots against the landscape. He was going at last...far, far away across the ocean. He would return with stories of things his people had never seen or heard of before.

As the *Atlantic* sailed from Sydney Cove, towards the sandstone headlands that formed the entrance to the harbour, Phillip had mixed feelings. There was so much unfinished business. Those misty mountains hadn't been conquered. They were still a mystery.

What lay on the other side? Was there a great inland sea?
Were there strange animals yet to be discovered?
Was there another civilization?
Or was there just a great stretch of nothingness?

As they sailed into the vast expanse of the Pacific Ocean, the first Governor of the colony of New South Wales and his Eora friend exchanged a nervous nod. What adventure, dilemma, mystery and discovery still lay ahead?

So many unspoken questions were yet to be answered.

THE END

Chief Surgeon
John White's house

Hospital

Marine Barracks where
Watkin Tench had lived

George Johnston's
first house

Reverend's house

Government
House

Storehouse

To Dawes' observatory

To Bennelong's house

A View of Sydney Cove, 1792

Author's Notes

All the people named in 'Stories of Life at Sydney Cove' really lived in or near the settlement from 1788; no names are invented or imagined. The stories in this book are about true historical events described in the journals, letters, diaries and reports of people on the First Fleet. To breathe life into the scenes, I have imagined conversations based on their accounts and the probable daily situations and relationships they shared.

Journal quotes and letters in shaded boxes are taken from actual journals or letters but have been simplified and shortened from the originals. For references to sources, see page 255. Also see the index and detailed notes in the non-fiction book, *Across Great Divides*, by Susan Boyer.

The Aboriginal words and phrases used in the stories are taken from the journals of Lieutenants William Dawes, David Collins & Captain John Hunter. Note that spelling varies. For information: **http://www.williamdawes.org/**

The courtroom proceedings of convicts in this book are taken from their court cases recorded at the Old Bailey, London.
For information: **https://www.oldbaileyonline.org/**

For a list of images in 'Stories of Life at Sydney Cove' see pages **253-254**

****

List of British (other than convicts) in 'Stories of Life at Sydney Cove'

Governor Arthur Phillip - leader of the First Fleet and first Governor
David Collins, Judge Advocate - Governor's secretary & judge in the colony
Lieutenant George Johnston - Governor's Aide de Camp, kidnapped Arabanoo
Reverend Johnson - clergyman to the colony, he & wife Mary adopted Boorong
Surgeon John White - Chief Surgeon in the colony, adopted Nanberry
Doctor George Worgan - sent letters to England, brought a piano to Sydney Cove
Captain John Hunter, Captain of HMS Sirius - kept a journal
Lieutenant Watkin Tench - kept a journal, befriended Aboriginal people
Lieutenant William Dawes - kept a journal, befriended Aboriginal people
Lieutenant William Bradley - kidnapped Bennelong & Colbee, kept a journal
Lieutenant Henry Waterhouse - gave eyewitness account of Governor's spearing
Lieutenant Ralph Clark - kept a journal & wrote letters to his wife Betsy
Mary Johnson - wife of clergyman, adopted Boorong
Lieutenant John Macarthur & wife Elizabeth - arrived free on Second Fleet

To download a **free bookmark** with a list of the people in
Stories of Life at Sydney Cove go to **www.birrongbooks.com**

List of Aboriginal people in 'Stories of Life at Sydney Cove'

Arabanoo - Aboriginal man, first kidnapped, later a friend of Governor Phillip

Nanberry - 9 year old Aboriginal boy, survived smallpox in Sydney Cove

Boorong - 14 year old Aboriginal girl, survived smallpox in Sydney Cove

Ballooderry - Aboriginal youth, Maugoran's son, Boorong's brother,
Nanberry's friend, he was buried in the Governor's garden

Maugoran - Aboriginal man, Boorong's father from Parramatta area

Barangaroo - Aboriginal woman, Bennelong's wife, buried in Governor's garden

Bennelong - Aboriginal man, friend of Phillip, Barangaroo's husband

Dilboong - baby daughter of Bennelong & Barangaroo, buried in Gov's garden

Colbee - Aboriginal man, Bennelong's friend & Nanberry's uncle

Daringa - Aboriginal woman, Colbee's wife, visited Elizabeth Macarthur

Patyegorang - young Aboriginal woman, friend & teacher to William Dawes

Pemulwuy - Aboriginal man who resisted British settlement

Yellomundee (also Yarramundi) - Aboriginal man living inland near Hawkesbury

Yemerawane - Aboriginal youth who went to England with Bennelong & Phillip

> In recreating stories of the interactions between British and Aboriginal
> people from 1788, I have relied on the accounts of British men who
> recorded what they observed and what the Eora told them. I am aware
> that they may have misinterpreted what they saw and heard however
> their accounts are the only written record we have of that period.

List of convicts in 'Stories of Life at Sydney Cove'

John Hudson - 13-year-old convict boy (was a London chimneysweep)

Elizabeth Hayward - 13-year-old convict girl, lived in Rev Johnsons' household

Dorothy Handland - listed as 82 years old, convicted for perjury

Isabella Rawson - convict teacher; gave birth on *Lady Penrhyn,* (see Richardson)

Henry and Susannah Kable - convicts (& baby), married at Sydney Cove 1788

Esther Abrahams - convict became life partner to Lieutenant George Johnston

James & Elizabeth Ruse - convict farmers at Experiment Farm, given 1st land grant

James Bloodworth - convict builder, advised Governor on building work

Thomas Barrett - convict engraver, sailed on *Charlotte*, hanged at Sydney Cove

William Bryant - convict fisherman, escaped in 1791 with Mary & children

Matthew & Elizabeth Everingham - convict farmers; was London attorney's clerk

John McEntire - convict game hunter; he was speared by Pemulwuy

William Richardson - married Isabella Rawson and set up first school

Acknowledgements

After publication of **Across Great Divides**: *True Stories of Life at Sydney Cove* I received positive feedback from teachers about its relevance to the Australian history curriculum. I'd like to thank those people for contacting me with their comments and encouragement because it inspired me to write this young reader version, *Stories of Life at Sydney Cove.*

I'd like to thank Christopher Tobin, Aboriginal cultural consultant, for reading the manuscript and providing valuable appraisal and advice on cultural aspects relating to Aboriginal content in the stories in this book.

I would also like to thank primary school teacher, Rhona Hughes for reading sections of the manuscript with her students and sharing their responses with me. I am grateful for her constructive suggestions for the books' application in the classroom. Thank you also to those students who took the time to give their opinions and reactions to the stories. I also want to thank primary school teacher Katherine Jackson for her appraisal and feedback on the educational aspects of this book.

I'm grateful to Jeanette Christian for proofreading the manuscript at various stages. As always, I'd like to thank my husband Len for enabling me to follow my passion and continue writing stories to inspire young Australians. I am deeply appreciative of his part in the production of this book. His input in enhancing and fine-tuning the final publication was invaluable.

I would like to thank marine artist, Ian Hansen for giving his permission for me to use images of his works, *'The First Fleet, Sydney Cove'* and *'Sydney Cove 1788'* to illustrate this book (pages 55, 58, 62, 78). I would also like to acknowledge marine artist, Frank Allen, for allowing me to use images of his paintings *'First Fleet in Sydney Cove'* and of the transport ships, *'Lady Penrhyn'* and *'Charlotte'* (22, 37, 54 & the title page). See a list of illustrations on pages 253-254.

I am thankful for the input of those mentioned above who have appraised and provided feedback on 'Stories of Life at Sydney Cove', however any errors are my responsibility. I would be grateful to know if any are found.

The journal quotes and letters in shaded boxes in 'Stories of Life at Sydney Cove' are from the original journals or letters but have been simplified and shortened from the original. For specific references to sources of quotes in journals & letters, see Index & Notes in *'Across Great Divides: True Stories of Life at Sydney Cove.'*

Images in 'Stories of Life at Sydney Cove'

Cover design by Susan Boyer (see imprint page for image details)

Title page: *The First Fleet Ships in Sydney Cove*, by artist Frank Allen

Historical Background page: *Route of the First Fleet,* map by Susan Boyer

Part 1: *The First Fleet entering Port Jackson, January 26, 1788*, E Le Bihan, SL NSW

Page 1: *The convicts near Black Friars Bridge*, by Pollard, Newgate Calendar 1795

Page 3: Small chimneysweep, *London Labour and London Poor*, Henry Mayhew 1840; background rooftops image: F.W. Odzbrook, 1880

Page 7: *Norwich Castle* from Charles Knight's *Old England: A Pictorial Museum* 1845

Page 11: Prison hulk, National Library of Australia

Page 15: *General Evening Post* by Susan Boyer, from the original newspaper article

Page 17: Old Bailey in *The Microcosm of London* Vol 2, London, Methuen & Co. 1808

Page 22: *Lady Penrhyn - Convict transport* reproduced courtesy of Frank Allen

Page 24: Flying fish (single) from *John White's Journal* published 1790, from Plate 52

Page 25 & 27: maps by Susan Boyer

Page 29: *18th century ship*, Willem van de Velde, National Maritime Museum, London

Page 31: *Aborigines spearing fish, others diving for crayfish, a party seated beside a fire cooking fish*, Joseph Lycett, 1817, National Library of Australia

Page 35: *Portrait of Captain Arthur Phillip RN (1786)* by Francis Wheatley, National Portrait Gallery, London

Page 37: *Charlotte,* with permission of artist, Frank Allen

Page 39: *Marine with hair braid* by Susan Boyer; *Aboriginal man with nose bone*, from Popular Science Monthly Vol 17, published by Appleton & co New York 1880

Page 42: *Watkin Tench* by unknown artist, 1800s, Mitchell Library, State Library NSW

Page 46: *Emu & Kangaroo*, drawings from Arthur Bowes Smyth's journal 1787-1789 (separate drawings: Kangaroo - Contents no.4; Emu - Contents no.5)

Page 48: *Charlotte medal* 1788, credited to Thomas Barrett, displayed in Australian National Maritime Museum (ANMM)

Page 50: *The First Fleet entering Port Jackson, January 26, 1788'*, E Le Bihan, SL NSW

Page 53: *The Founding of Australia, Jan. 26th 1788* by Algernon Talmadge, SL NSW

Page 54: *The First Fleet Ships in Sydney Cove,* with permission of artist, Frank Allen

Page 55: *The First Fleet, Sydney Cove,* with permission of artist, Ian Hansen

Page 58: *The First Fleet, Sydney Cove,*(detail) Ian Hansen

Page 62: *Sydney Cove, 1788,* with permission of artist, Ian Hansen

Page 64: *Aboriginal man with nose bone,* (see details for p. 39)

Page 65: *Layout of Sydney Cove,* Susan Boyer, source: *nla.gov.au/nla.map-nk276*

Page 70: *Aboriginal implements* from *John White's Journal* pub'd 1790, from Plate 63

Page 74: *Variegated Lizard*, from *John White's Journal* published 1790, from Plate 38

Page 77: *Snake*, from *John White's Journal* published 1790, from Plate 46

Page 78: *Sydney Cove 1788*, with permission of artist, Ian Hansen

Images in 'Stories of Life at Sydney Cove'

Original journals & records cited in *Stories of Life at Sydney Cove*

Convict court-cases at London's Old Bailey: www.oldbaileyonline.org/

Experiences of **Ralph Clark** and convicts aboard *Friendship*, and at **Sydney Cove**, see 'Journal and Letters of Lt. Ralph Clark 1787 – 1792'. See a digital copy: http://adc.library.usyd.edu.au/data-2/clajour.pdf

Experiences of **Henry Kable** and family, see newspaper accounts published in the *London Chronicle*, Dec 2-5, 1786 and 21- 23 July, 1789.

Experiences aboard *Lady Penrhyn* and at **Sydney Cove**, see 'Journal of **Arthur Bowes Smyth**: Surgeon Lady Penrhyn 1787-1789'. See http://acms.sl.nsw.gov.au/_transcript/2015/D36405/a1085.html#a1085009

Experiences aboard *Charlotte*, at **Botany Bay** and **Sydney Cove** see **Watkin Tench**, '*Complete Account of the Settlement at Port Jackson*'. Digital copy: http://setis.library.usyd.edu.au/ozlit/pdf/p00044.pdf See John White's journal: http://gutenberg.net.au/ebooks03/0301531h.html

First Fleet, **Aboriginal people** & life at **Sydney Cove**, see Secretary **David Collins** '*Account of the English Colony in New South Wales', Volume 1 & 2*. Online: http://gutenberg.net.au/ebooks/e00010.html

Contact with **Aboriginal people** and life at **Sydney Cove**: see journal of **George Worgan**: http://adc.library.usyd.edu.au/data-2/worjour.pdf See also journals and letters of **Governor Arthur Phillip**: http://acms.sl.nsw.gov.au/_transcript/2007/D00007/a567.html#a567004 http://gutenberg.net.au/ebooks/e00101.html

Aboriginal word-lists by **William Dawes**: http://www.williamdawes.org/

Aboriginal people at **Sydney Cove** (including Boorong & Nanberry) see **John Hunter's** journal: http://adc.library.usyd.edu.au/data-2/hunhist.pdf

Aboriginal people at **Sydney Cove**, see **William Bradley's** journal: http://acms.sl.nsw.gov.au/_transcript/2015/D02131/a138.html#a138009

Reverend Richard Johnson's letters about life at Sydney Cove: http://www2.sl.nsw.gov.au/archive/discover_collections/history_nation/terra_australis/letters/johnson/

Elizabeth Macarthur's letters about her voyage and life at Sydney Cove: http://gutenberg.net.au/ebooks13/1302011h.html

The spearing of **Governor Phillip** by an Aboriginal man at Manly, see **Henry Waterhouse's** account recorded in William Bradley's journal: http://acms.sl.nsw.gov.au/_transcript/2015/D02131/a138.html#a138009

See links to online references above at www.birrongbooks.com

About the author

Susan Boyer is an Australian author with over twenty non-fiction titles in print. She has a teaching background spanning twenty five years in the area of English language and literacy, however her passion for Australian colonial history is evident in her recent publications (see below).

Following her teaching career, Susan is now a full-time researcher, writer and presenter with a focus on Australian history. Since 2014, she has presented author talks in schools, given radio interviews and published articles on the importance of true, inspirational stories from Australia's past. She is listed with *Reading Australia* as part of their 'Authors in Schools' program to promote Australian stories.

www.susanboyer.com.au
or
www.birrongbooks.com
www.boyereducation.com.au

****

Other books by Susan Boyer
History titles
'Across Great Divides: True Stories of Life at Sydney Cove'
'People in Australia's Past: Their Stories, Their Achievements'
For curriculum links and teaching resources for the above history titles, see:
www.birrongbooks.com

English Language and Literacy titles
Rhyming Stories
English Language Skills
Word Building Activities for Beginners of English
Spelling and Pronunciation for English Language Learners
Understanding English Pronunciation
Understanding Everyday Australian (series)
Understanding Spoken English (series)

Across Great Divides:
True stories of life at Sydney Cove

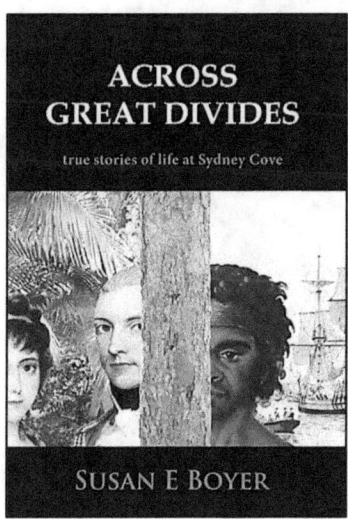

'Across Great Divides - true stories of life at Sydney Cove', brings to life the diverse experiences of people living in the precarious circumstance of Australia's first penal colony. The stories are relayed through a non-fiction narrative.

The stories also give voice to the dilemma of the Aboriginal people challenged by the unexpected arrival of white people to their land.

All the stories relate to the people and actual events as recorded in journals, letters and official reports of the First Fleet.

Read the different perspectives of military men volunteering for a tour of duty in the remote colony.

The book contains bibliography, index and detailed notes on original sources.

Australian history - Non-fiction - RRP $26.95

ISBN 9781877074424

Available from all good book stores and online at
www.birrongbooks.com

Australian curriculum links and free teacher resources @
www.birrongbooks.com

Susan Boyer is available for library and school visits to talk about the stories in her books.

© Birrong Books is a division of www.boyereducation.com.au